DARK DREAMERS

BEING A TEENAGER IS A CURSE

Thank you Craig!

LEON MITCHELL

DARK DREAMERS

BEING A TEENAGER IS A CURSE

Created and Written by
Leon Mitchell

Cover Illustrations by
Nick Ashton

Dark Dreamers

Being a Teen is a Curse

Created and Written by Leon Mitchell.

All stories characters, associated stories and narratives within this book written
and created by Leon Mitchell.

United Kingdom, first edition print 2025.

© Leon Mitchell.

Illustrations copyright © Leon Mitchell.

Illustrations by Nick Ashton

Initial original concept art, characters faces by Cherry Sweet

ISBN-Paperback: 9798290131665

ISBN-Hardbackback: 9798290454627

Publisher Catalogue Number: CLPLMDD2502

Leon Mitchell is passionate about helping to preserve the worlds forests.
Only paper from legal and sustainable forests is used. Please think before
printing.

WHATEVER YOU DO...
DON'T TURN THE LIGHTS OFF!

Contents

Chapter 1

Sentence of Suffering

It was late July when the four of them—Lila, Cassie, Morgan, and Emma—were vomited out from the shadowy confines of the youth detention centre. They squinted into the jaundiced light of the setting sun, the scent of disinfectant and despair still clinging to their clothes.

Freedom felt like a phantom limb, an ache for something that wasn't really there. In the centre, they had forged a sisterhood from the jagged shards of their shared pain, a bond of scar tissue and whispered rage. By some cruel joke of the system, they were all released on the same day.

Lila, the group's reluctant leader, had found the book. It was in the detention centre's library, a place that smelled of slow decay, wedged behind brittle legal encyclopaedias. It was bound in something that felt unnervingly like human skin, cool and supple. The legend was that it belonged to a girl who had gone mad within those walls, who clawed her own eyes out and simply vanished from her locked cell. They said she didn't escape, but was devoured by her own nightmares.

Drawn by the book's sickly sweet promise of

power, they began to practise its secrets in the grim, damp bedsit the probation service had found for them. At first, it was trivial—charms for protection, whispered curses at their wardens. But the book was a hunger, and it taught them to be hungry too.

One moonless, suffocating night, they decided to perform the ritual described on the final, stained page: a binding of dreams, a shared escape. They drew a sigil on the floorboards with a mixture of salt and ash, each adding a drop of blood that beaded black in the centre. As they chanted the words, which felt like swallowing glass, the air grew thick and heavy, the pressure of the deep ocean. It smelled of ozone and grave dirt. Light bulbs flickered and died. They didn't fall asleep; they were dragged under, into a shared darkness.

They awoke in a forest. A sky the colour of a day-old bruise pulsed overhead, and silver moonlight bled through the canopy of skeletal, weeping trees. The ground beneath their bare feet was soft and yielding, like flesh. This was no sanctuary. A wet, dragging sound was always just behind them, and whispers slithered from the oppressive darkness between the trees—not just their fears, but twisted parodies of their deepest hopes. They realised, with a dawning, icy dread, that their demons hadn't just followed them here.

They had been waiting.

Morgan was the first to break. The branches of a great oak writhed and knitted themselves into the towering shape of her father, his face a mask of fury. But it wasn't his voice that accused her; it was the thorns that grew from his wooden skin, which detached and flew at her, embedding themselves in her flesh, each one a whisper of her failure.

Cassie was trapped in a hall of mirrors, but the glass reflected versions of her committing atrocities she had only ever imagined, their eyes burning with a triumphant evil. Then, the reflections began to move, their fingers pressing against the other side of the glass, which bulged like a soap bubble, threatening to burst.

Emma was hunted by the ghosts of her past, but they weren't ethereal. They were waterlogged and bloated, crawling from a black, swampy bog, their mouths full of mud as they gurgled her name, their dead hands reaching to drag her down into the filth with them.

Lila, fighting to keep a scream from tearing her throat apart, found herself back in the isolation room. The walls weren't stone; they were compacted, screaming faces, their silent agony a physical pressure. The air was dust, the dust of powdered bone and dried tears, and she was forced to breathe it in, choking on despair.

Desperation led them towards a discordant, off-key lullaby that echoed from the forest's heart. There, stitched into a throne of roots and human bone, was the mad girl from the library. Her face was a preserved, rotten mask, her eyes empty sockets from which silverfish crawled. She was the warden of this prison. She smiled, a gesture that split her cracked lips. The only way out, she whispered in their minds, was to feel a pain greater than the one that trapped them.

In a final, frenzied showdown, they fought back. Morgan tore the thorny effigy of her father apart with her bare hands, screaming as splinters the size of needles drove deep into her palms. Cassie smashed the mirrors one by one, letting the shards slice her arms, accepting the monstrous reflections as her own. Emma let the gurgling figures pull her under the mud, embracing their cold, dead weight until they dissolved around her. And Lila, with bloodied fingernails, clawed at the walls of screaming faces until they crumbled into dust, leaving her kneeling and gasping in the wreckage.

They awoke on the bedsit floor with a single, unified scream, the stench of the nightmare forest still in their nostrils. They had splinters in their hands, deep scratches on their arms, and mud under their nails. The book was buried that same day, deep in the earth, a desperate, pathetic attempt to end it. For a single afternoon, they allowed themselves to hope.

But that night, Lila was woken by a syrupy whisper that coiled around her brainstem.

There, at the foot of her bed, dripping with fresh soil and nightcrawlers, was the book.

An unseen force slammed her down onto the mattress, which suddenly felt like soft, damp earth. Her eyes rolled back into her head as she was pulled back into the nightmare forest. The others were already there. They weren't just hanging; their bodies were impaled, woven into the thorny, ever-growing branches like living tapestries. Their limbs were stretched and tangled, their mouths open in silent, unending screams, their eyes wide and staring, forced to watch each other's torment for eternity. All control had been ripped from them. Their bodies were no longer their own, but puppets for the Warden to arrange into new, beautiful sculptures of pain.

This time, there was no release date. They were not prisoners. They were scenery. Sentenced to an eternity of suffering, not in a cell, but as part of the very nightmare that had promised them escape.

Chapter 2

The Whispering Halls

It was a crisp autumn afternoon when the students of Friarwood Secondary School first noticed that strange things were happening around them. The fallen leaves were scattered all around the courtyard; the air was smoggy and thick with the scent of wet earth and decay.

But for the teens of Friarwood, it wasn't just the change of seasons that felt different this year. There was an eerie tension in the air too, a sinister, whispering undercurrent that no one could ignore.

Lena, a second-year student at the school, had been hearing things—soft murmurs in the hallways, the tap of shoes when no one was around, scratches on the walls randomly appearing. At first, she thought it was just her imagination, or maybe a draught making the old school building creak.

After all, Friarwood was a hundred years old, with its peeling walls, old splintered doors and dim, flickering lights. But when Lena was walking through the hallway, it happened again. She was walking down one of the more run-down hallways after school when she heard it—clear as day. An uninviting voice, faint and distant, but unmistakably a whisper. "Lena…" it called out. She spun around, her heart thudding in her chest, but no one was there and the hallway was empty.

The hairs on the back of her neck prickled, and she hurried to the nearest exit, her footsteps echoing unnaturally loud in the silence.

The next day, Lena noticed that other students were acting strangely. Her best friend, Emily, had been in the same hallway that morning and she heard the whisper too. Emily's face was pale, she barely spoke all day, and she wasn't the only one. Several others had heard it too: Jake from chemistry class, Sarah from history, even Mr Owens, the grumpy janitor, who was always quick to dismiss any nonsense. But he'd started muttering about "the spirits of Friarwood."

By the end of the week, more and more students had reported hearing voices or seeing strange shapes moving quickly in the halls. Some claimed they saw shadows that weren't there, or figures lurking in the corners of classrooms with hollow eyes, only to disappear when looked at directly. Everyone was on edge and becoming more frightened. Some of the teachers tried to keep everyone calm, saying there was nothing to worry about.

Lena decided to investigate this further and try to figure out what was going on. She spent her lunch breaks in the school library, searching through old yearbooks and dusty files about the history of Friarwood. What she found chilled her to the bone. Friarwood wasn't always a school. Before it was built, the land had been home to an old mansion, owned by the wealthy and mysterious Gillard family. The mansion had burned down in a strange fire, and there were rumours that the Gillards were involved in dark rituals.

The fire killed everyone inside, but the fire department had never figured out the cause or found the bodies. It was as if the flames had erupted from nowhere, consuming the mansion in minutes. Eventually, it was all forgotten about and ignored, as no answers could be found.

The school was built soon after, but ever since, strange things had happened. Students reported hearing voices, seeing things in the corners of their eyes, and some even claimed to have seen the ghostly figures of the Gillard family wandering the halls. It wasn't until Lena's discovery that anyone realised that Friarwood's foundation was built directly over the remains of the mansion, and possibly the bodies. One explanation was that the land itself was cursed, steeped in the dark energies of the fire. And now, those energies were waking up to haunt the students and staff.

That year on Halloween night, Lena and her friends decided to be brave and confront whatever was haunting the school. Armed with just torches and their courage, they snuck into the school after hours when it was late.

The air was thick and heavy, almost suffocating, as they wandered the familiar yet unsettling halls. Every creak of the floorboards echoed like a warning; they were scared but determined to find out the truth.

As they reached the old basement door, the temperature dropped sharply. Their breath misted in the cold air now covering them. The whispers started again—low, dark and coming from the shadows below. But this time, they weren't just words. They were a strange and evil-sounding chant, a beckoning, pulling them closer. Lena swallowed her nerves and led the way, the others worried but trailing behind her in hesitant silence. They descended into the basement, where the air smelled of damp earth and decay again.

Suddenly, the torch glass cracked; it flickered and went out, plunging them into complete darkness. Panic surged through the group as they gripped hold of each other. They took deep breaths, settled, then Lena pushed forward, relying on her eyes to adjust to the darkness. But then, they saw it.

At the far end of the basement, a figure appeared. It was tall, gaunt, and skinny, with hollow eyes and a cruel smile. It was one of the Gillards—Lena could tell by the old-fashioned clothes it wore, the same ones from the black-and-white photographs she'd seen in the library. The figure raised a hand, and the whispers grew louder, more urgent. They were in complete panic, terrified and screaming inside.

"Leave now," the figure rasped, its voice echoing around them. "You should never have come here." Lena's heart raced, and she grabbed Emily's arm, pulling her quickly towards the stairs. But the figure didn't move. Instead, it seemed to multiply, stretching across the walls, its twisted faces grinning from the shadows. Panicking, they ran up the stairs, but the door slammed shut before they could escape. They were trapped.

Suddenly, there was a loud crash—like a door breaking open. The hallway outside erupted in chaos, and the ghostly whispers reached a deafening crescendo. But then, something unexpected happened. The figure in the basement wailed in anguish, and the walls began to shake. A cold wind howled through the corridors, rattling windows and knocking over bookshelves.

In that moment, Lena realised the curse of

Friarwood wasn't just the spirits—it was their desperate need to escape, to have their suffering recognised. The school wasn't just haunted. It was alive, feeding off the fear of those trapped within it. With one final, spine-chilling scream, the spirit of the Gillard family seemed to implode on itself. The basement door swung open, and the air grew still. The group ran, not daring to look back. The next day, the students of Friarwood noticed a strange calmness in the school. The whispers were gone. The shadows had receded. But something had changed. The school still felt alive, but it was quieter, as if the spirits had finally been given rest.

Lena, however, would never forget what they had seen that night. Friarwood was no longer just a school—it was a place of forgotten tragedy, and the spirits of the past were always waiting, lurking just beyond the walls.

And as the years passed, Lena's whispers began again. But this time, they came from the walls of her own home, tormenting her each night. It wasn't over; it was just the beginning. And Lena was about to suffer, as the ghosts of the past tried to come into the world and use her as a gateway, until her last breath.

Chapter 3

The Girl Who Vanished

It was a cold cloudy afternoon when Emma Harold disappeared. The bell had just rung out, signalling the end of another monotonous school day at Greenwell secondary school. Emma, a quiet 14-year-old with long, dark hair and a collection of tatty books always tucked under her arm, had been walking home like she did every other day.

But that day, something felt different, something was wrong. Her best friend, Lily, had called out to her from the school gate, but Emma didn't turn around this time.

Instead, she walked on, her footsteps soft against the pavement and moving quickly. Lily thought nothing of it at first, assuming Emma was just lost in thought or didn't hear her. But when Emma didn't show up at school the next day, it was odd, but not immediately alarming either.

Emma had a tendency to skip classes from time to time when her anxiety got the best of her. But, by the end of the week, she was still not in and the school began to panic. No one had seen her, not a single trace.

For days, the search was frantic. The police

scoured every corner of the town trying to find her, but there was no sign of Emma anywhere. Her parents were beside themselves with worry and panic and feeling sick, and Lily couldn't change the feeling that something was horribly wrong. Yet, with every passing week, the hope that Emma would be found dwindled.

The media and the town began to move on, but the empty desk in Room 203 remained a constant reminder of the girl who had vanished. Lily was heart broken and struggled to understand what happened, but eventually had to come to terms with it.

3 years later—It was the last day of our final school year, when the news broke. The small town of Greenwood was hopeful again. Because Emma had been spotted, walking alone through the woods just outside town, barefoot, disheveled, and looking like she hadn't aged a day since she disappeared.

It was impossible—how could a girl vanish for years and return without a single sign of any change at all? But there she was, in the flesh, her eyes wide and empty, like she had just stepped out of a dream, or even a nightmare.

Lily, now older herself, stood in shock as she watched Emma's return unfold. Her heart raced as Emma was escorted into the school building, pale and trembling, but still somehow familiar. She didn't seem to recognise anyone. Her parents were there too, crying, but Emma looked at them with confusion as though she didn't know who they were.

"I don't remember anything," Emma said repeatedly when the authorities questioned her. "I don't know where I've been. I woke up in the woods, and I... I don't know."

Her voice trembled as though she was lost inside her own body, trying to find herself and escape her pain. Lily tried to speak with her, but Emma's gaze passed over her like a stranger, as though she were looking through her rather than at her. "Lily?" she whispered, but there was no recognition in her voice. "Who are you?"

Over the next few weeks, the town tried to make sense of it all and felt deeply connected to the case, they wanted answers and to understand what happened. Although Emma had returned, she was different, something had happened to her. Her once-bright eyes were dull, her laughter had fallen silent. Eventually she came back to school and the people around her tried to return her life to some sort of normal. But she would wander the halls of the school, staring out of windows as though waiting for something and ignoring everyone.

There were whispers. Some said she had been

taken by something… something that had changed her inside and out and made her their obsession. Others thought she had been running away from something, but no one really knew or could they explain the gaps in her memory, the void where the missing years should have been.

One evening, Lily decided to visit Emma at her house. She wanted to help again, to bring her friend back, but something in the air felt off when she arrived. The house was quiet, too quiet. No one answered the door, but it was open, so Lily let herself in. What she found was worse than anything she could have imagined.

Emma was standing in front of a cracked mirror, her face pale, gaunt and ghostly, her fingers tracing and being cut by the glass as if she could feel something—or someone—on the other side of it. Her lost and torn reflection, though, wasn't quite right. It was blurry, shifting like water, and Emma's eyes—her eyes were different and distant. They were… darker and cursed. There was something behind them, something that wasn't her.

"Emma?" Lily whispered, stepping closer to help, Emma didn't turn, her fingers still tracing the glass and filling the cracks with her blood.

"I don't know where I've been, Lily. But I know I was alone. And I know they want me back." Lily took a step back with worry and caution.

"Who, Emma? Who wants you back?" Emma's lips curled into an eerie, almost imperceptible smile.

"It's not over. Not yet." Suddenly, a cold wind swept through the room, slamming the door and extinguishing the lamps, leaving the two girls in darkness. The air grew thick with an unsettling and choking energy, and Lily could feel something ancient pressing down on her, suffocating her too, she felt like she couldn't leave.

She reached out for Emma, but her body seemed to flicker in and out of reality, as if she were no longer fully there. When Lily reached for her again, Emma's skinny hands vanished, and a low, sinister voice filled the room,

"I'm not the same. I'm never going back to who I was." Lily's heart pounded as the temperature in the room dropped, her breath forming in the cold haunted air. She backed away, her eyes never leaving Emma, who now stood in front of the mirror, her reflection laughing at her—distorted, twisted, wrong.

"I can feel them in me," Emma murmured, they own me, her voice barely audible. "They're calling and pulling me. I... I have to go, forever, to be tortured, twisted and tormented, forever.

Then, Lily felt something smother her and take

her breath away, she passed out. The next morning she woke in her bed, not knowing what was real or what was a dream. She tried to explain what happened to the authorities and Emma's parents, but no-one believed her.

Her parents said that night they did not hear or see anything and that Emma was safe in her bed. But reality soon kicked in when they realised Emma was taken, she is gone again. No one knew where she was or where she had vanished this time, and the authorities or her parents never found a trace.

The only thing left was the lingering chill that seemed to haunt and curse the house, and the sense that Emma had never truly come back—she had only returned to take something with her, something that had been waiting for her all along.

Her parents eventually moved out, they could no longer live in the place where their daughter was stolen from them. One day, her dad disappeared too, some say he left the country, others say he was taken away to be with Emma, but no one really knows.

Emma's mum ended up in a mental health hospital, she could never speak again, but every day she would look in the mirror and press her hand on it, as if she was waiting for Emma, seeing her. And now, the town waits, just waits for the girl who went missing too hopefully return again, unsure of what she will bring back with her next time, if anything.

The mirrors, though… the mirrors seem to know what really happened, maybe Emma is trapped within them, caged in a life of painful horror. They hold a dark secret, a secret we will never know and they will never share, even when they break and shatter.

Chapter 4

The Noise in the Attic

It was the kind of night that was perfect for a sleepover. The air had a chill, the moon hung heavy in the sky, and the creak of the old, splintered house seemed to fit the mood perfectly.

Jessica and her friends had been planning this sleepover for weeks—pizza, movies, and scary ghost stories were all part of the group plan for the evening. The house was an old, run-down Victorian-style home belonging to Jessica's grandparents.

It was big, dark, and full of strange shapes and rooms that seemed to stretch on forever. It was the ideal place to get lost in the shadows and for things to get spooky very quickly.

The six friends arrived for the sleepover, filled with excitement and nervous energy, and gathered in the living room, spread out on sleeping bags with bowls of sweet treats.

The flickering white glow of the TV screen cast eerie shadows on the walls as they watched a frightening horror movie that no one was really paying attention to. Giggling and laughter echoed in the room, but when the movie reached a particularly tense moment, the conversation suddenly shifted.

"Okay," said Claire, the self-proclaimed ghost story expert, "who wants to hear a true story?" The room fell quiet, all eyes fixed on her, eager to hear something scary.

"It's about this house," she began, her voice low and teasing. "My aunt once lived in a place like this. Big, old, kind of terrifying, and maybe even haunted. But the worst part wasn't the way it looked. It was the disturbing noise."

Jessica shifted uncomfortably on her sleeping bag and tucked her hands in. She'd heard the stories before, but there was something about being in this house that made her feel even more uneasy. She'd always heard the rumours about the attic—how it was always too cold up there, like a sharp chill, and it was difficult to breathe, but how people said they could sometimes hear footsteps, stepping slowly from above.

"What noise?" Rachel asked, her voice sounding shaky.

"The noise came from the attic," Claire whispered, leaning in closer to her friends, as if to make the story more secretive. "At first, it was just small sounds. Like… scratching and tapping. Like something was trying to get out, or get someone's attention, maybe.

But as time went on, the sounds became louder and more intense. Thumping, like someone was pacing back and forth, impatiently waiting for something."

Jessica's heart skipped a beat, but she tried to keep her voice casual so she didn't appear scared. "That's just a bunch of old nonsense, it really is. The wood in these old houses creaks all the time."

But Claire wasn't done. "No, Jess. That's what my aunt thought at first too. But then, one night, she heard it. Clear as day—someone whispering in the attic."

Suddenly the room grew cold, and even the faintest breeze seemed to stop; you could hear the heartbeats of the group. Jessica's mind began racing. She had always felt weird about the attic. The door to it was located at the end of the hallway, hidden behind an old, cracked mirror.

Her grandparents had always warned her to never go up there, saying it was just "storage and nothing to see." But things were quickly starting to make sense; something about that warning felt really off. Too… specific.

Suddenly, there was a sound that broke the silence. A soft scrape from above. Everyone froze.

"Did you hear that?" Rachel whispered, her

mouth dry and voice tight with fear.

"I… I didn't hear anything," Jessica said, but the words felt hollow and meaningless, even to her. Then there was another strange sound. A thud, followed by a faint, unusual shuffle. It was coming from the attic above.

Jessica's heart raced. "It's probably just the wind or a rat, maybe," she said quickly, but her words were unconvincing to the others.

The rest of the group was already staring up at the ceiling, eyes wide and horrified at the grim possibilities that lay before them.

"I think it's coming from the attic too," Claire said, her voice trembling now with fear.

"Stop it, Claire," Rachel snapped. "You're just trying to scare us."

But Claire wasn't looking at them anymore. She was staring at the staircase leading up to the attic, fixated and obsessed with it. The noise had stopped, but the air in the room now felt thick and choking, like it was pressing down on them with a crushing sense of unforgiving evil.

"Let's just go check it out," Claire suggested, her voice taking on a strange, determined tone that was out of character. "What if it's just a bird scuttling around in its nest or something?"

Jessica stood up and wasn't able to stop herself.

She didn't know why, but she felt an overwhelming sensation in her body to go and investigate; it was like she was being pulled towards the fear and the unknown.

"Fine. We'll go up together," she said, trying to sound braver than she really felt. They huddled at the bottom of the stairs.

The old wooden steps creaked and cracked under their weight as they made their way slowly up the narrow, creepy staircase.

The air grew colder as they climbed, making their hairs stand up on the back of their necks. The faint smell of old dust and something else— something musty—filled their noses and scratched their throats.

At the top of the stairs, Jessica hesitated for a moment. The shadowy attic door loomed in front of them, dark and closed.

"Maybe we should just go back," Rachel said, her voice quivering now with fear. But Claire had already stepped forward. "I'm opening it," she whispered, her eyes reflecting in the low light.

With a loud groan, the door swung open. The attic was dark, save for the dim light from the window spilling in. Boxes were stacked haphazardly, and old cobwebs clung to the rafters. But then, something caught Jessica's eye. A strange shape, moving in the far corner. Her breath was caught in her throat. "What is that?"

The shape didn't move again, but the air around them grew heavier. A faint whisper brushed against Jessica's ear, barely audible: You shouldn't be here.

Before anyone could react, the door slammed shut behind them, cutting off their escape.

The sound of footsteps—slow, deliberate—began echoing across the attic floor. But no one was there. Jessica's pulse quickened. She grabbed Claire's arm. "We need to get out of here. Now!"

But Claire was frozen, staring at something in the corner again. There, in the shadows, something was watching and staring at them. Something that wasn't supposed to be in the attic.

A weathered face, pale and twisted with a grin too wide for its exposed skull, stared back at them. Suddenly, the door flung open again with a bang! The girls didn't wait another second.

They ran down the stairs, hearts pounding in their chests, and when they reached the safety of the living room, they didn't speak a word. Their throats were tight and it was hard to breathe; no words would come out.

They just sat there, staring at each other, unable to move as a strange force wrapped around them, keeping them still. All they could do was watch each other in fear, the sound of their choking breaths the only thing they could hear. Then above them, the noise started again.

A slow, deep thump. Thump. Thump. It was coming from the attic. And this time, it wasn't stopping. It was coming for all of them, and there was no escape. It came down the stairs slowly and moved into the room, silent, ghostly and with bad intentions.

All they could do was wait and watch each other meet their fate. One by one, they were eaten alive.

And the last thing that Jess saw after watching all of her friends suffer in extreme pain, was the wide-open grin spread across that evil face coming towards her too.

Chapter 5

Evil Waters

The sun had just dipped below the horizon as the boat glided through the water, a perfect evening for a party. A group of teenagers, excited and carefree, danced to the music pumping out from the speakers, their laughter echoing across the ocean surface. Irresponsibility echoed all around them as they played party games and flirted with one another, life seemed endless. They'd been planning this night for weeks—a party on the water, far from the rules of parents, of school, of everything. It was freedom, they thought, just a few hours out on the open sea to get up to whatever they wanted. But little did they know, they were not alone.

Their sense of direction started to become blended up with all of the excitement they were having, the boat drifted freely as they had forgotten to lower the anchor. "Are we lost yet?" Jake, the joker of the group said, he laughed and leaned over the side, staring into the endless expanse of dark water below him. He saw something move, but it disappeared into the deep, he decided not to tell the others. "Come on, we've been out here for like an hour. How can we be lost?" said Lily, his best friend, she rolled her eyes, but her voice wavered just a little. She noticed that she couldn't see any land around the boat.

The water around them was calm, but it was nearly impossible to tell if they were heading in the right direction. In the fading light, everything looked the same—just water and sky merging together into an inky void quickly closing further every minute. The boat's captain, a friend of Lily's older brother named Matt, had assured everyone they were still in the safe zone and that he knew the waters well. But as the night stretched on, the party began to die down and the atmosphere shifted into more of a dark feeling of doom.

The music seemed quieter now, the laughter a little more forced and uneasy. Someone noticed that the stars above had scattered in strange, unfamiliar patterns, and the cool breeze had turned into a sinister haunting wind. "Matt, how much further?" Lily asked, her voice tight now. She hadn't been paying attention when they set out, but a sinking feeling had taken root in her chest.

The mood was changing, and not for the better. Matt checked the compass on the boat's dashboard, his brow furrowing. "Uh, it's weird… the needle's acting off. It's spinning in circles."

"What do you mean, off?" Jake asked, suddenly

serious and concerned. Matt shrugged with no answer, but the unease in his eyes was unmistakable.

"I don't know. It's never done that before." It just won't seem to pick up North.

The group fell silent and looked around, each of them starting to realise something was terribly wrong. The sound of the engine seemed unnervingly loud now, almost as if the boat was being pulled in a direction it wasn't meant to go. It felt cold and damp and tiredness was setting in.

"Guys," Lily said, looking around. "I don't think we're where we're supposed to be." Jake tried to joke, but it didn't come out right. "It's just the wind. Maybe we're just drifting a bit." But no one laughed.

The water had changed, too—where the dark expanse of ocean had once felt endless and freeing, it now seemed suffocating, as if something was watching from beneath the surface ready to take them. It was scary with a feeling of hopelessness. At one point the dark water almost felt like it was dark red, like an ocean of blood all around them with no escape.

Minutes passed like hours and time seemed to stop, soon even the horizon vanished entirely, leaving them in a deep black void. The boat's lights flickered and there was a sound of an electrical circuit failing. Suddenly, the engine sputtered and then died completely. "Matt?" Lily asked, her voice small and now insignificant.

Matt scrambled with the controls pressing buttons and dials, but nothing happened. "What the hell? It's gone. We've got no power everyone." Panic set in as they realised they were stranded, alone in the middle of the vast terrifying ocean that felt like it was about to punish them, and there was nothing they could do about it. The night was ghostly and eerily still, and the water felt so much more unfriendly now, the once gentle waves suddenly unnerving and haunted.

Someone turned on their phone, but there was no signal. Nothing at all, this was the same for everyone. Jake tried to start up the engine again, his hands shaking with nerves. "What's going on? This isn't happening. We're just freaking out over nothing." He said, but knew that something bad was going to happen.

Deep down, everyone else also knew that something was terribly wrong, so they huddled together tightly. Then came the noise. It started as a soft creak beneath the boat, so subtle that at first, they thought it was just the wood groaning. But then it grew—low, almost guttural, like something was scraping against the hull. Something large.

"Matt?" Lily whispered, but Matt was staring into the water, his face pale. "Matt, what is that?" In the darkness, shapes began to move beneath the surface. They were too large to be fish—too slow, too deliberate. The water around the boat began to ripple unnaturally, the surface turning more blood red and shifting as if something massive was circling them, watching them, preying on them.

And then the cutting whispers started and it wasn't the wind. It was something else, something inhuman, a voice that slithered in the dark, curling around their minds like a cold jabbing fog. Each of them heard it—it turned soft, then unintelligible murmurs that sounded like promises, but also like warnings. They couldn't make out the words, but they knew, somehow, that it wasn't friendly and only had bad intentions for all of them.

Their minds started to wander uncontrollably, playing over painful scenarios of how they might face death, it was torturing. Jake swore under his breath, his eyes darting wildly. "Did you hear that? I—I swear I heard something." "I—" Lily's voice trembled.

"I don't know what's happening, this is awful, I want to go home. We need to get back. Now." But the boat didn't move. Matt pulled at the steering wheel, desperately trying to restart the engine. His hands were slick with sweat.

"This isn't happening. This isn't happening." The water beneath them churned violently, as if something was rising from the depths. A sharp, jagged shape broke the surface—an enormous, pale, twisted form, with eyes like dark, empty sockets, staring up at them.

And that's when they knew. They should have never left the shore, the darkness was always going to come for them. The whispers grew louder now, distorted, clawing at their minds and stabbing at their thoughts, and in the distance, other strange shapes began to surface—slow, deliberate, like the shadows of creatures that had been waiting beneath the water for years.

The boat rocked violently as the dark forms circled closer, their hollow lifeless eyes in clear view under the moonlight. They were there to cause fear, pain and suffering. Their merciless and evil intentions cut around the boat and climbed higher onto the decking.

One by one the group of friends were impaled by the jagged forms but left to live for a few moments to look at each other in shock and fear. They were slowly pulled one by one beneath the blood stained water, as their breath ran out and water filled their lungs, and their eyes closed forever.

As the last of the party's curdling cries for help faded into a haunting deep silence, the ocean closed in around them to hide its secrets. And they were never heard from again.

To this day, the coast guard still receives reports of a boat that went missing on a calm night, with no signs of a wreckage though. Just the whisper of a haunted wind, and the sounds of drowning as something ghostly stirs in the deep.

Chapter 6

Trapped Dreams

Five teens are sat in a circle, eyes dull with the weight of their shared histories. The room smelled like antiseptic and stale air, the sterile environment of the group therapy centre offering no comfort. Each of them had their own scars—some physical, others deeper, hidden under layers of ingrained defence. They had all been offenders in their own right—stealing, fighting, hurting people—each crime telling the story of someone who had been broken by a world that never seemed to care. They had all been thrown into the gutter to survive and learn the ways of deception.

There was Jake, the quiet one with dark eyes and a heavy dishonest stare. His past was a sketchy patchwork of bad decisions. Then there was Margo, loud and sarcastic, trying to mask her insecurities with tasteless humour. Dorian was the brooding one, always angry, with an aggressive temper he could never control. Leah, a confused girl with no memory of her life before the system, and finally, Ivy, who had the quiet air of someone who was always listening but never speaking. Something had taken her long ago; she was almost lifeless.

They met every week in group therapy, all of them marked and judged by their offences, forced to confront their wrongdoings. But tonight felt different. It had been six months since their release from the youth detention centre, and after all the failed attempts at normalcy, they had become friends—strange, broken friends—but friends nonetheless.

"I swear," Ivy said quietly, "this place is the only thing keeping me from… losing it."
The others looked and nodded in agreement. They weren't friends because they wanted to be; they were bonded by their shared experience in a system that had broken and failed them all. But not just the system, life had failed them too.

"I wonder," Leah mused, "if we all just… stopped trying to fit into the world, and let the world just… go crazy. What would happen?"

Jake, the most reserved, shot her a glance. "You've been reading weird books again, Leah." Leah just shrugged, a small, mysterious smile tugging at her dry lips. "No. Just thinking about things. Like… if dreams were more real than we thought. What if we could change things in them?"

Margo rolled her eyes. "Please, stop with the crazy talk." But Leah didn't seem to hear her. "What if we could… cross into each other's dreams?"

"That's a bit out there, even for you," Dorian said, snorting. He leaned back in his chair, his arms aggressively crossed together, the faintest smile tugging at the corner of his lips. "Are you trying to get us all in trouble again, Leah?"

But Leah was in a trance, staring at the floor, her voice low. "No, I'm serious. I've had dreams about places… that felt real. And people I knew… but they weren't people I knew in real life. What if it's something we're supposed to do? Something we need to do."

Leah revealed a book she had been reading; it was full of dark dreams and curses of nightmares and suffering. She explained to the group that she had found it hidden under a loose floorboard in her bedsit and had been practising and reading the scriptures—and that it possibly belonged to the man who was killed in that room, but no one ever knew how it happened.

There was a long pause, the group unsure how to respond. For a moment, everything felt like it could just fade into the mundane noise of group therapy. But then, something scary and strange happened.

It was Ivy, looking down at her phone, who noticed the odd symbol etched into the wood of the table like an old scar. It was barely visible, an old symbol scratched into the surface, something that didn't belong in the sterile therapy room. Her fingers touched and traced the symbol lightly.

"What the hell is this?" Ivy murmured. Dorian glanced at it. "It wasn't here before. What did you do, Ivy?" "I didn't—"

Before anyone could react, the symbol pulsed. The lights in the room flickered, and the air grew thick and heavy, as if the walls themselves were closing in with a crushing sensation. A sudden chill swept through them all, and the sound of dark, shattered, and painful voices seemed to rise from the depths of the room.

"W-What's happening?" Margo stammered, her voice trembling for the first time in weeks. The group's tension broke when the sound of a door creaking echoed across the room. But it wasn't the door to the therapy room. It was much deeper and darker, from somewhere inside their minds. The floor beneath them seemed to slither, and without warning, they were no longer sitting in the sterile room.

They were in a dark, vast place—an endless void of nothing, stretching farther than they could comprehend. They stood in a circle, no longer physically in their therapy room, but surrounded by an abyss.

"What the hell…?" Jake whispered, his voice echoing unnaturally in the void. His choking breath came out in panic, his hands shaking.

Leah stepped forward, her eyes wide, her voice barely above a whisper. "We did it. We unlocked it." "Unlocked what?" Dorian shouted out, but his voice faltered as he too noticed the sudden shift. His heart pounded in his chest.

"I think… we've unlocked the curse," Leah said. "We can travel between our darkest dreams. And now, we're all in this together."

Before anyone could respond or even think, the void around them rippled, and the air grew thicker with a suffocating presence over them, like something was waiting, watching. Suddenly, the group was pulled apart by a supernatural force, each one yanked and dragged into their own separate nightmare. It was terrifying; a sense of death was everywhere.

Jake found himself in a dark, never-ending alleyway, the jagged, bone-crushing walls slowly closing in around him. Shadows whispered his name and tormented his thoughts. Margo was in a room full of mirrors of horror, each one reflecting her worst fears.

Dorian was drowning, trapped in a vast ocean with no way out, only the weight of the deep pulling him down deeper, never to breathe or see another soul again. Every time he inhaled the salty water, he would wake back up and repeat the nightmare again.

Leah was crunched up and locked in an iron cage, with blood-stained figures with smeared faces watching from beyond the bars as she suffered, jabbing her with sharp iron rods. Ivy was surrounded by empty, shifting faces that were hollow and cracked, all of them mimicking her own relentlessly without ever stopping.

They were all trapped, but not just in their own darkest fears that never ended. They were trapped in each other's nightmares too, and they could feel each other's pain over and over again. Each of them screamed for what seemed like an eternity, their voices muffled by the strange, dream-like barrier separating them. Their voices were lost to the darkness they had unlocked, never to be heard again and never to be given another chance.

But through it all, there was one thing that bound them together—the symbol on the table, and it also appeared on the book. It was the bloodiest curse. And they realised, as the dark forces pressed in on them, that they couldn't escape the nightmare unless they faced the darkest parts of themselves. Together.

But there was one difficult question that lingered between them all as they struggled to survive in their shared dream world of unbearable suffering:

How would they reach each other, and what if they never woke up?

Chapter 7

The Curse of the Midnight Unicorn

It was the night of the full moon when a group of friends found themselves at the edge of the woods. A social hiking day they didn't want to end had led them to extend their time together and venture off track. The mist had crept in from the mountains around them, swirling in eerie patterns as it clung to the trees like a shroud.

The teens, suddenly drawn closer together by a tale of an ancient, forgotten maze hidden deep within the forest, and a strange creature that waited for anyone who became lost. They had no idea what they were about to face.

Kayla, the leader of the group, was often the brave one. She had read about the labyrinth in a dusty old book at the local library—about the tormented unicorn that roamed its endless twists and turns. It was said that anyone who ventured into the maze would be relentlessly hunted by the creature, unable to escape its pursuit until the very end.

"Come on, it's just a story. What could go wrong?" Kayla said, smirking as she led the group deep into the forest and toward the crumbling stone archway that marked the entrance to the maze.

"I don't know, Kayla… this place gives me the creeps," muttered Ethan, the sceptic, always quick to joke about the paranormal. "What's the worst that could happen though, maybe none of us make it out alive?"

A cold wind shuddered through the trees, sending a shiver down their spines.

"Whatever happens, we stick together," Kayla said, though her voice lacked the usual confidence she had. There was something about the maze that unsettled her too, something she couldn't quite put her finger on. Maybe it was the strange markings etched into the stonework at the entrance point. They stepped through and into the darkness to begin with, their flashlights cutting through the gloom, casting strange shadows that danced on the walls of the narrow, crumbling corridors. The air grew damp and soggy, and the ground beneath them seemed to shift with every step, as though the maze itself was alive and changing their direction.

"Look at these walls," said Mia, Kayla's best friend, her voice tremulous. "They're… covered in scratch marks." She pointed to the jagged lines that ran up and down the stone.

"Old carvings," Kayla shrugged. "Probably from explorers who got lost and never returned." Kayla was trying to ease the situation with humour, but it didn't work.

But it wasn't the walls that made their blood run cold. It was the sound—the distant, echoing clip-clop of hooves, faint at first, then growing louder with every step they took. They all realised they had walked so far into the maze that they were unable to trace their steps back to the entrance, and the walls had become too high to scale or climb.

Ethan stopped, his face pale. "You see that?" A large overpowering shadow passed across the walls. The hairs on the back of their necks stood up. From the dark, a pair of sinister glowing eyes appeared, followed by a silhouette of something much taller than them—something with a long sharp spiralling horn.

The creature was a ghostly mysterious unicorn, but not like any they had ever imagined in fairy tales. Its coat was black as midnight, its mane twisted and wild like a tempest. Blood-red eyes locked onto them, a malicious gleam burning in its stare. The unicorn's horn shimmered with an eerie, unnatural light, and it pawed at the ground, as if preparing to charge.

Before anyone could react, the creature lunged forward, its hooves pounding the stone, the sound vibrating through the floor. It was faster than any horse, its speed almost supernatural. They all screamed and sprinted and had no time to think, but the unicorn was relentless. Its gaze followed them no matter where they ran.

"Split up!" Kayla shouted, her voice breaking. "We have to lose it!" But the maze was a labyrinth, twisting and turning, with no clear path to follow. Each turn only brought them deeper into its heart, where the air grew thick and oppressive.
Every time they thought they had found an exit, they were led straight back into the same dark corridor; the feeling in their stomachs was sickening.

The unicorn's hooves never stopped echoing, always just a step behind—constantly stalking them with no emotions at all.

Kayla found herself alone. Her heart pounded in her chest as she dashed around another corner, her breath ragged. She could hear it now, closer than ever—clip-clop—and then the unmistakable sound of a screeching cry, like a battle cry from a creature in pain.

A low growl sounded behind her; she could hear its hot breath clashing with the chilly thick air. She spun around. There it was. The unicorn stood at the end of a narrow pathway, blocking her way. It was no longer just a creature of legend—it was real, and it was here to kill.

"Kayla…!" Ethan's voice echoed through the maze, distant, faint. She turned back, but the maze was an impossible matrix of dead-ends and traps, all twisting in on themselves like some cruel trick. The unicorn's eyes burned into her, and it was coming closer.

She had no choice. She just couldn't think straight and ran straight at the creature. It reared up, hooves striking the air, but in that moment, she leaped sideways, tumbling down a small slope into an old, hidden chamber. Kayla gasped for breath, her body scraped and bruised from the fall. But the creature was right behind her.
It hovered over her, its dark form swallowing the light.

The unicorn's breath was hot against her neck, and in that moment, Kayla knew: the maze wasn't just a place of myths—it was a trap, a prison designed to keep anyone who entered from ever escaping.

And now, it had her. The last thing she heard was the sound of its hooves scraping the stone as the creature prepared to strike and impale her.

The others never saw her again; they were left to think about how her fate ended. They each searched the maze for hours, but the walls seemed to close in on them at every turn, each step deeper into the trap. And just as Kayla had fallen, so too did they—one by one, lost forever to the maze. Their screams echoed through the endless corridors, never to be heard by anyone. And to this day, the maze has never been seen again. Explorers have tried to find it, but nothing is ever found, just thick dense forest.

But the legend has it that the maze is out there somewhere, hiding its secrets, waiting. And The Midnight Unicorn still roams the labyrinth, its red eyes glowing in the darkness, hunting for anyone who happens to enter, especially teens on school hiking trips.

No one ever leaves, no-one is ever found, not even in death.

Chapter 8

The Library of Forever

It was an ordinary Tuesday afternoon when 16-year-old Emma found herself alone in the school library. The hushed silence of the rows of books was usually comforting, but today it felt heavy, expectant, as she nestled into one of her favourite armchairs. Outside, the sunlight was a sickly, jaundiced orange, staining the pages of the book in her lap.

She'd pulled a tatty old book from a forgotten shelf, its leather cover cracked and faded like old skin, the title long since scoured away by time. Curious, Emma flipped it open. The paper was brittle, and the first page was blank, but the second was filled with looping, spidery handwriting, scratched into the page with a desperate hand: "To those who dare open these pages, beware. This is not an escape. It is an entrance."

Emma gave a short, nervous laugh. It was probably some weird old story with a dramatic warning. She started to read, but as she did, the words on the page began to blur and writhe. The sounds of the library—the soft rustle of paper, the ticking of the old clock—faded into a low, distant hum that vibrated from the book itself, up her arms, and into her bones. Before Emma knew it, she felt a violent pull. The book shook in her hands, a malevolent power thrumming within it.

She tried to scream, but the sound was choked in her throat, a dry, useless gasp. Panic seized her as the world around her spun, the walls of the library twisting and distorting, stretching into impossible, nauseating angles. Her vision clouded, and a force like a physical blow slammed into her, as if she were being torn apart and stitched back together again. With a sickening jolt, she fell to the ground.

Emma scrambled to her feet, every inch of her screaming in protest. The air was crisp and damp, the smell of rot and ancient mildew heavy in her nostrils. The library was gone, replaced by a dense, primeval forest. Twisted, skeletal trees loomed above her, their branches crooked like broken fingers, choking the last of the light from the sky. The faint glow of a distant firelight flickered between them, casting long, dancing shadows.

"What the hell?" she shouted, her voice trembling. The book was still clutched in her hands, its pages now open to a new chapter, one that hadn't been there before. "Once trapped, you can never return. The hunt begins at nightfall."

Before Emma could react, she heard a skittering

sound behind her. She spun around, but there was nothing there. The wind cut through the trees, carrying a distant, chilling laugh that seemed to mock her terror, playing with her. Her heart hammered against her ribs. She turned to run, but something—or somethings—were already in motion, their forms darting between the trees like glitches in reality. Emma's breath caught in her throat as she realised they weren't human.

They were faster than anything she'd ever seen, with eyes that glowed with cold, intelligent malice and limbs that bent at unnatural angles. They lurked just at the edge of her vision, always watching. She hadn't even had a chance to process where she was, but already, she was prey.

As nightfall descended, the forest came alive. The creatures drew nearer, their eyes gleaming in the darkness like hot coals. Emma could hear their footsteps, light but deliberate, a dry patter on the dead leaves, closing in. She tried to run, but her feet felt like lead, her legs burning with a fatigue that went beyond the physical. The path ahead was a lie, the trees seeming to shift and writhe with every turn to confuse her on purpose.

She glanced down at the book. The page had turned again, the words stark and black against the parchment: "The hunt has begun. You will run until your soul is ragged."

Terror, pure and absolute, gripped her. She wasn't just in another place; she had been pulled into a story, a twisted narrative where she was the quarry in a never-ending, torturous pursuit.

The creatures were close now, so close she could smell the decay on their breath. One, a tall, gaunt figure with pale, cracked skin, stepped into the firelight, its lips pulling back into an impossibly wide grin, revealing rows of jagged, needle-like teeth. It was ecstatic, feeding on the fear radiating from her, savouring her utter solitude.

Emma screamed and turned to run, but there was no escape. No matter how fast she ran, the creatures followed. She could hear them, smell them—feel the cold void of their presence just behind her. They were always close, flitting in and out of the trees, a constant, teasing torment. They never allowed her to rest.

When her eyes grew heavy with exhaustion, one would dart close enough for its cold, dry finger to trace a line down her spine, a violating touch that sent jolts of revulsion through her. It never ended.

The night stretched into an eternity. With every ragged breath, the world seemed to fold into itself, repeating, as though she were running through a maddening loop. The trees blurred, the shadows stretched, and the book never left her hands. It continued to turn its pages, each one a new verse in her personal hell.

A sudden, searing pain flared on her chest. She tore at her shirt and looked down. New words had appeared, not on the page, but burnt into her own skin, the flesh red and raw around the letters: "You cannot leave. You will run forever. The book is your prison."

As Emma finally accepted the horrifying truth—that she had become a permanent character in this nightmare, trapped in a chase that would never end—her scream was lost with the echoes, swallowed by the forest. She would run until the end of time, her agony a silent whisper within the dark embrace of the pages that had consumed her, forever.

Chapter 9

The Other Side of the Bell

It started on a normal Monday, but the air already felt thin and grey. For seventeen-year-olds Jenna, Jake, Lily, and Ben, the lunch bell had just rung. They gathered outside by the ancient oak tree in the schoolyard, their laughter sounding brittle against the unnatural quiet of the day.

Lily had found an old, leather-bound scroll in the school archives, wedged between a stack of dusty encyclopaedias in a forgotten cupboard. The pages were weathered and fragile, the words written in a scruffy, ancient script that seemed to squirm on the page. She'd brought it to the group, thinking it was just a strange artefact, maybe a prank. But when she opened it during lunch, a deep unease coiled in the pit of her stomach.

"Hey, check this out," Lily said, her voice a little too bright.
Ben squinted at the cover. "What is that? A list of spells or something?"

"Probably some weird role-playing game stuff," Jake shrugged, though he didn't look convinced.

"Let me see," Jenna said, taking the scroll. As her fingers brushed against the cracked leather binding, a sharp, cold burn shot up her arm, as if the scroll itself was branding her. Wincing, she rolled it fully open. The symbols on the page seemed to pulse with a faint, sickening light, even in the watery daylight.

"That's... not normal," Lily murmured, her voice shaking.

Before anyone could respond, the ground beneath them shifted. A low, grinding sound filled the air, a sickening sound that vibrated in their teeth and bones, coming from nowhere and everywhere at once.

The sky above them curdled, the grey clouds darkening to a bruised purple. A violent wind erupted, swirling around their bodies like a predator, forcing them back against the trunk of the tree.

Lily's voice was a choked gargle. "I think... I think we've unlocked something."
"Something bad," Jenna finished, her heart hammering.

The scroll pulsed with a blinding, malevolent light. They screamed, shielding their eyes as the ground beneath their feet didn't just give way—it shattered. They were plunged into a nauseating vortex of screaming colour and crushing pressure, falling for what felt like forever.

When they hit the ground, it wasn't earth. It was

a cold, hard surface that seemed to vibrate with a life of its own. They looked around, dazed, and saw that they were no longer in the schoolyard. The world had been remade into a nightmare.

The sky above was a sheet of pitch black, dotted with cold, dead stars that were arranged in impossible, geometric patterns. The air was thick with the sickly-sweet, metallic smell of old blood. Twisted, skeletal trees clawed at the blackness, their branches reaching for them like desperate fingers trying to escape. There were no sounds—no birds, no wind. Only a deafening, pressurised silence that pushed in on them.

"Where are we?" Jake whispered, his voice swallowed by the oppressive quiet.

"This isn't our world," Jenna muttered, her eyes wide with terror.

That's when they heard it. A low, wet, gurgling growl, coming from somewhere deep in the suffocating darkness. A shadow, impossibly large, detached itself from the trees. They didn't wait to see what it was. They just ran, pure instinct driving them into the alien woods.

Hours, or maybe days, bled into one another. The world was an endless, shifting labyrinth of dark trees and stalking shadows. No matter how far they ran, they couldn't escape. The very landscape seemed to be a living trap, herding them deeper into a perpetual nightmare like cattle.

It wasn't until they stumbled upon a shard of a broken mirror leaning against a tree that they began to understand the true horror. In its reflection, they saw their own faces, but they were impossibly older. They looked thirty, maybe more, their faces gaunt, their skin scarred, and their eyes hollowed out with a lifeless, soul-deep exhaustion. The reflections stared back, not with recognition, but with a terrifying mixture of hatred and pity.

"What is happening to us?" Lily cried, her voice breaking.

"Time… it works differently here," Ben stammered.

Before anyone could answer, they heard it again. The heavy, deliberate tread of something immense. The shadow that had been hunting them was drawing closer.

They ran, legs aching, breath tearing from their lungs, until finally, after an age of torment, they burst through the trees and found themselves at the base of a huge, stone doorway. It was carved with the same writing scriptures from the scroll and seemed to pulse with a faint, sickly light.

"This is it," Jake gasped. "We can get out." But as they lurched towards the door, the world began to scream. The ground cracked open around them, and the sky tore itself apart, unleashing a light so absolute it erased everything.

The next thing they knew, they were standing in the schoolyard again, the lunch bell ringing in the distance. The sun was shining. It was as if no time had passed at all. But everything was wrong.

They looked at each other, their faces pale, their clothes impossibly dirty and torn. A bone-deep weariness clung to them, the phantom weight of lost years.

"I… I feel different," Lily said quietly.
"Yeah," Ben agreed, his voice hollow. "Like we've been gone for decades."

"How long were we….?" Jenna started, but they all knew. It was only moments here, but it was a lifetime somewhere else.

The curse of the other world had been unlocked. And as they stood there, trembling, they realised something even more terrifying: they hadn't escaped. It had followed them back.

The bell rang again, and this time the sound was a discordant, mocking toll—a death knell.

When they looked at the school, the windows were no longer just glass. For a split second, they saw distorted, skeletal shapes moving behind them. The faint, grinding hum from that other place shuddered in the air, whispering their names.

They knew then. The hunt wasn't over. Their own world was now the hunting ground, and there was nowhere left to run. Their fate was to keep running, until eventually their bodies collapsed and caved in, with no one to help them. And worst of all, no one would ever know where they went. They were taken, forever.

Chapter 10

The Ghostly Teacher

It was a blustery autumn afternoon when rumours about Mrs Hawthorne, the new history teacher at Bulmershe school, began to fester. She was a brittle, quiet woman with waxy skin, always seen in long, black dresses, as though perpetually in mourning. Students whispered about her strange mannerisms: how she never smiled, how her eyes seemed to stare just beyond them, as if watching something ghastly unfold in the space they occupied. And then there were the strange happenings in her classroom.

At first, it was just a feeling. Her lessons were strangely captivating, but a suffocating silence fell upon the room whenever she spoke. The air grew colder whenever she passed by, a grave-chill that clung to the skin long after she was gone, and the lights would flicker violently every time she entered or left. But it wasn't until a few weeks into the semester that things took a darker turn.

One day, during the middle of class, Mrs Hawthorne asked the students to write an essay on the history of ghosts in folklore. Everyone thought it an odd topic, but they complied. That's when things started to unravel.

After class, a student named Mielè stayed behind to ask for help. As she stepped closer to her desk, the classroom door slammed shut with a final, booming echo, plunging the room into a sudden, muffled silence. She spun around to see her standing in the corner, her eyes glowing with a faint, phosphorescent light. The room was now freezing, the unnatural cold of a mausoleum, and Mielé's breath plumed in the air.

"Mrs Hawthorne?" she called out, her voice sounding small and dead.

She didn't respond. Instead, she turned her head with a slow, crackling sound, and her face—pale and sharp, with deep hollows where her eyes should be—seemed to flicker and warp, the features momentarily dissolving into a skeletal mask. Mielé froze, a scream trapped in her throat. She lunged for the door, but the handle wouldn't turn. The lights above sputtered, casting shadows that crawled on the walls like living things.

"History… is not just about the past," Mrs Hawthorne murmured, her voice like the dry rustle of dead leaves. "It's about what never leaves us."

An oppressive sense of dread filled the room, so heavy it felt hard to breathe. Mielé backed away, unable to tear her eyes from her. Then, with a sudden, impossible speed, she was gone—vanishing into the deepening shadows. The door handle slowly turned with a loud creak, and the door swung open by itself.

Mielé stumbled out, gasping for air. She was pale and shaking, but when she looked back, the classroom was empty and normal. There were no flickering lights, no strange cold. It was just a room again.

The next day, Mielé tried to tell each of her best friends–Emily, Katherine, Emily D, Gem and Evie. But every time she began to speak, she felt her throat tighten, as if invisible, icy fingers were squeezing it shut. They laughed it off anyway; no one believed her. But then, more students started to notice the oddities. Faint, tortured voices lingered in the halls near her room. A search of the school archives revealed Mrs Hawthorne had supposedly been teaching at Bulmershe school for over twenty years, her face appearing unchanged in old staff photographs that no living teacher remembered being taken. Even stranger, none of the current staff could recall when she had started.

The rumours began to spread like a contagion: Mrs Hawthorne wasn't just a teacher—she was a ghost. A spirit trapped in the school, never ageing, never leaving. Some students swore they saw her wandering the halls late at night when rehearsing for a school play, her long black dress sweeping silently behind her as she vanished through solid walls.

Others claimed they'd hear her faint, disembodied voice when they passed her classroom, but when they opened the door, the room was always empty. The few students who dared to stay after class with her couldn't stop shaking. They said the closer you got to her, the more you felt as if you were sinking into another world, a cold, grey place where time had no meaning.

As the weeks wore on, the once-vibrant school grew quieter, a creeping rot setting into its very foundations. Teachers spoke in hushed tones about Mrs Hawthorne, exchanging nervous glances whenever her name was mentioned. None of them would go near her classroom after hours.
No one dared ask Mrs Hawthorne about the strange occurrences, but the most unsettling theory lingered at the back of every student's mind—what if she had never been alive in the first place?

The bell would ring, students would file out of the classroom, but there was always that lasting feeling—that Mrs Hawthorne, the ghostly teacher, was always watching them from the corners of every room, her hollow eyes waiting for the next lesson.

And sometimes, if you stand in the empty corridor long after the day is done, you can just barely make out the faintest whisper through her closed door—an invitation.

"Come in and learn, let me teach you… what it is to become history."

Chapter 11

The New Girl

When Sophie walked into Brooklands school on the first day of the new term, no one could have guessed what would happen. She wasn't anything extraordinary to look at: messy brown hair, wide, innocent eyes, and a pale face that was too fragile-looking for her age. She moved through the halls like she was floating, as though she didn't quite belong.

Her powers had always been something she couldn't explain. Since childhood, things had happened around her. Objects would move without explanation and people around her would feel… different. Her family had taught her to hide it, to suppress it. But a new school meant new people, and for Sophie, that meant something darker was about to unfold.

The first sign of trouble was small—an accident in the classroom. Sophie had been sitting alone at a table, studying, when she overheard a conversation between two girls in the next row. One of them, Rita, was mocking Sophie's worn-out rucksack, laughing with her friend, Sara. Sophie didn't think much of it, until the laughter started to grow more intense, more cruel.

Suddenly, Rita's face froze in a twisted smile, her hands trembling. She looked over at Sara, but her words were unintelligible—just twisted, moaning sounds. Sara's eyes widened in panic as she backed away, but Rita's voice was louder now, and sharper.

"Why… Why can't you hear it?!" Rita screamed. Other students were staring, but Rita didn't notice. Her face contorted in confusion and fear as she clawed at her head, her mouth opening and closing as if trying to scream but unable to.

Sophie stood up, feeling a tingle in her fingertips. It wasn't her fault, not really. But something—something dark—spoke to her, coaxing her to pull more from within. She didn't stop herself. And just like that, Rita's screaming stopped. Her eyes glazed over, and she stumbled back, collapsing onto the floor. The room fell into a deep, unnerving silence.

The teachers arrived shortly after, but by then, Rita had gone completely mute, staring blankly ahead as if something had broken inside her. By the next day, whispers about Sophie had spread. They said she was cursed, that something was wrong with her. But none of them knew the truth. Sophie wasn't cursed—she was just beginning to understand what she could do. And it terrified her.

As the weeks passed, Sophie noticed the changes.

People around her started acting… strangely. At first, it was subtle—a small, misplaced outburst in class, a sudden loss of focus, a temper flare from the most even-tempered of students. Teachers who had once been kind and patient became irritable and short-tempered, snapping at students for no reason at all. Life at Brooklands school became unbearable with tension, and Sophie could feel it pressing on her chest, heavy and suffocating.

One afternoon, during class, it all came to a head. Sophie was sitting at her desk when she overheard a group of popular girls gossiping about her, calling her "weird" and "creepy." They weren't even trying to hide their disdain any more. Sophie felt her heart race, her palms begin to sweat. She couldn't help herself. She focused all her energy on the gossip—the noise growing louder and louder in her head. She just wanted them to stop, to leave her alone.

Suddenly, one of the girls, Mia, let out a piercing scream and grabbed her head. "What… what's happening?! Why is everyone talking?! I can't stop hearing them!" she cried, her voice rising to a frenzied pitch. The other girls turned to her, their faces twisted in confusion, their eyes darting back and forth as if they could see invisible figures. One by one, they joined in, shrieking as though they were being tortured by voices only they could hear.

Sophie stood up, shaking. She hadn't meant for this to happen. But there was no going back now. The chaos around her was feeding into something deep inside her—a darkness that felt too powerful to resist. She turned away, her footsteps eerily silent as she left the room. The hallways were empty. The school was eerily quiet, save for the maddened wails that echoed from the classrooms and were now drawing attention.

By the time Sophie reached the main exit, the entire school had erupted. Students were running in all directions, shouting, pulling at their own hair, clinging to each other in panic and pain. The madness had spread like a virus with no mercy. Teachers were no exception, and the once-thriving school had been reduced to a place of fear, hysteria, and madness. There was no sanity left, just mental torture and disorder.

Sophie stood at the edge of the car park, watching as the world she'd just stepped into crumbled. She hadn't meant to cause all this. But it was too late now. The voices had stopped talking, but their influence still lingered in her mind, praising her for what she had done.

And as she walked away, a sickening thought crept into her head: What if it wasn't the school that was broken? What if it was her all along?

Eventually, the school was closed down. Everyone who had been inside was never able to speak again or close their eyes; all they could do was just stare, stare into an empty, lifeless void that now consumed their lives. They were all placed in mental institutions around the country, never to return to their former lives. But somehow when you looked into some of their eyes, you knew they were thinking, and they understood you, but they were unable to say anything.

Sophie continued to live her life as normal, knowing she had sent the entire school crazy. The wind howled around her as the sun set, casting long, twisted shadows over the broken remnants of Brooklands school. And Sophie—alone, powerful, and mad—knew that the madness had only just begun.

Chapter 12

The Glimpse

Nina had always been curious and suffered from impulsive behaviour. The world around her felt like a blur of fleeting moments, and she longed for something that would give her a sense of control over the chaos. So when she saw an advert for a new social media app called "Glimpse," promising to show users a glimpse of their future, she couldn't resist.

"See what's coming. Predict your tomorrow," the tagline read.

It was revolutionary, the ad claimed. With a simple scan of your face, the app would analyse your behaviour, patterns, and life choices, and generate a personalised, digital prediction of your future. It wasn't like those fake fortune-teller apps—this one had the backing of top scientists, and Nina was hooked.

She downloaded it immediately. The interface was sleek, simple, and oddly… comforting. Nina hesitated for only a moment before entering her details: name, age, a clear selfie. The screen flickered as the app processed her data. And then, the future appeared before her eyes.

It was unsettling at first—a series of brief snapshots: her graduating high school, travelling to Europe, starting a career. But the last image sent a bone-chilling sensation down her spine. It was of her standing in the middle of a busy street, looking down at her phone, as a car sped towards her. She was frozen in place, completely unaware of the danger. Nina's heart pounded like a drum. Could this really happen?

She quickly dismissed the thought. It was just an app, right? Just a prediction, and not a guarantee after all. And she had time—years, even. The app didn't seem to know everything; it couldn't. At least, that's what she told herself.

But as Nina scrolled through her social feeds, she saw that her friends were using the app too. One by one, they shared their predictions, each more unsettling than the last. Her best friend, Zoe, posted hers next. It was a picture of her smiling in a park, but the next snapshot was chilling. Zoe was lying motionless on the ground, a shadowy figure standing over her. The caption read: "Zoe's future. A dangerous fall."

"Hey, do you think this thing is real?" Nina messaged Zoe.

Zoe responded with a nervous laugh, posting another image: a car crash. It was a scene she knew all too well—her dad's car, her own face twisted in terror. "It's not real, right? It's just a stupid app," she typed. But Zoe couldn't shake the feeling that something was off. Nina could tell. The next day, Zoe was in an accident. A fall from the seating stand during a football game, just like the app had predicted.

She was unconscious for hours, but she made it through, this time. Her doctor and teachers couldn't explain why she had been so clumsy that day— especially given how athletic Zoe normally was.

Nina began to worry. Then came Jake's turn. Jake was one of the quieter kids at school, but the app still predicted his future with uncanny detail. His first snapshot showed him laughing at a party, surrounded by friends. But the next image was disturbing: Jake lying in an alleyway, covered in bruises, his phone crushed underfoot. The caption: "Jake's future. A violent encounter."
When Jake saw his future, he shrugged it off. "It's not real. Just some creepy algorithm."

But it happened. The very next weekend, Jake was attacked after a party, beaten so badly that he ended up in the hospital with broken ribs and a fractured arm. The police couldn't find the attackers. It was like the prediction had come true, as if the app had shown them exactly what would happen.

And then it happened to Nina. Her prediction arrived just as it had before—standing in the middle of the street, a car speeding towards her. But this time, the image lingered longer. The caption was clearer than before: "Nina's future. The time is near." Panic set in.

Nina couldn't sleep. She couldn't eat. Her world revolved around the app, and it was becoming more and more apparent that it was predicting something terrible. Her friends, too, began growing paranoid. Zoe refused to leave the house. Jake started avoiding streets where cars sped past. But they all knew— they all saw their futures.

Then Nina received a new notification from Glimpse.

"Your time is close." Nina's heart skipped a beat. She couldn't just wait for the inevitable, could she? She had to do something. She had to stop it. Desperation led her to search for any clue, any hidden message that could explain what was going on.

After hours of digging through forums, reading user reviews, and even contacting the creators, she found an unsettling theory. Some believed the app was more than just an algorithm.

It was using an ancient form of predictive

magic—an unknown force that fed on human lives and linked their choices with the future it showed them. The more users that interacted with the app, the stronger the force became. A dark, dangerous force that had begun to feed on the lives of those who used it.

Nina shared her discovery with Zoe and Jake and sent it to the local newspaper. They agreed to take a risk. The three of them would go to the source—the company behind the app. If they could destroy it, they might be able to erase the future it had shown them.

They made their way to the headquarters, a tall, glass building in the heart of the city. But when they arrived, the building was locked down, security tight. No one was allowed inside. It was then that Nina realised the horrifying truth: the app wasn't just predicting their futures—it was controlling them. The more they tried to escape their futures, the more the app manipulated them and sent them down a rabbit hole.

And as they walked away from the building, on the final step—standing on the road near the headquarters' locked doors—a familiar message flashed on Nina's phone: "The future is irreversible."

A sharp sound echoed in Nina's mind. The app

had one final prediction for her: "Your end is here." As Nina looked around in horror, she knew that no matter what they did, the app had already decided their fate. She looked to her left, where a heavy, speeding truck hit her without braking, causing her to be torn apart on impact. Her phone lay there on the floor with a cracked, flickering screen as her life was taken.

It displayed one final message before the screen died too:

"The future, it seemed, wasn't something you could change. It had already been written, please leave a review for the app."

Chapter 13

The Mirror in the Bathroom

It was an ordinary Tuesday when Mia and her friends decided to skip class and hang out in the derelict section of their school. A specific rumour had been swirling for years about the girls' bathroom on the third floor. It was a place sealed in the school's memory, a place you didn't go. It wasn't just old; it was wrong. Teachers never confirmed the story, but their tight-lipped refusals to deny it were far more terrifying. Being caught near it meant immediate suspension, no questions asked.

"Have you heard about the mirror?" Lucy whispered, her voice getting lost in the cavernous hallway where the fluorescent lights buzzed and flickered like a dying breath. Mia rolled her eyes, a flicker of irritation masking a deeper unease. "The one where if you stare into it long enough, you see something… off? Yeah, I've heard the ghost story."

"It's more than that," Lucy insisted, her voice trembling. "I heard it doesn't just show you something wrong. It shows you what's inside you. The ugliest, most broken part. And then it keeps it."

Of course, they laughed it off with the brittle confidence of teenagers. But the story, now spoken aloud in the forbidden corridor, began to gnaw at them. Curiosity was a hook, and it was pulling them in.

The bathroom door groaned open into an eerie, tomb-like silence. The air was stagnant and cold, smelling of damp decay and forgotten things. A single, bare bulb spasmed overhead, casting twitching shadows across the grimy, tiled walls. But it was the mirror at the far end of the room that held the silence. It didn't belong there. It was a full-length antique, its silver frame ornate and tarnished with black, creeping stains, like frozen ivy. It seemed to drink the light from the room, its surface dark and deep, less like glass and more like a pool of still, black water.

A collective shiver went through them. "You first, Mia," Lucy challenged, her bravado gone.

Mia stepped forward, her footsteps echoing unnaturally. She stood before the glass, meeting her own eyes. For a moment, it was just her. She blinked. In the mirror, her reflection blinked a fraction of a second too late. A cold knot tightened in her stomach. She shifted her weight to her left foot. The girl in the glass remained perfectly still, her eyes locked on Mia with a terrifying, vacant intensity.

"See anything creepy?" Jason asked, his voice

sounding distant.

"Nothing," Mia lied, her own voice a croak.

Then, it changed. The reflection—the thing wearing her face—slowly, deliberately, raised its hand and pressed its palm flat against the inside of the glass. Its eyes were no longer vacant; they were filled with a frantic, screaming terror. Its mouth opened, a perfect 'O' of silent agony. It was her, Mia realised with a wave of nausea. It was her, trapped in there, begging for help.

A cold that had nothing to do with the room's temperature swept over her. She stumbled back, but the terrified reflection stayed put, its hand splayed against the glass. Mia's own body felt heavy, her movements sluggish, as if she were moving through water. She reached out, her trembling fingers hovering just before the cold surface.

And then the face in the mirror changed again. The silent scream vanished. The terror in its eyes was replaced by a look of ancient, chilling malice. The mouth twisted upwards into a smile that was not her own. It was a predator's smile, thin-lipped and cruel, stretching just a little too wide at the corners.

"Guys?" Mia whimpered, trying to turn to her friends, but she couldn't tear her eyes away. They were all staring into the mirror now, but their faces were slack, their eyes glazed over. They saw nothing. They were just staring at a dirty old mirror. They couldn't see the monster wearing her face.

The reflection in the glass, the smiling thing, tilted its head. Its gaze was possessive. It slowly raised its other hand and pointed, not at Mia, but through her, at her friends. A voice slithered into Mia's mind, a sibilant whisper that sounded like dead leaves skittering across pavement. You should have come alone.

Panic erupted in her chest, hot and sharp. "GET AWAY FROM IT!" she screamed, her voice tearing through the silence.

It was too late. The thing in the mirror slammed its palm against the glass, and the sound was not of flesh hitting glass, but of a hammer hitting stone. The surface of the mirror rippled. Mia felt an impossible, icy grip seize her own wrist. She looked down in horror. The reflection's hand was phasing through the glass, its fingers impossibly long and cold, wrapped around her arm, pulling her forward. Its grip was like iron.

"It's got me!" Mia shrieked, her feet sliding on the grimy floor as it dragged her towards the glass. Her friends snapped out of their trance, their eyes wide with terror as they saw Mia being physically pulled into the mirror's unyielding surface. Her arm was already gone, disappearing into the dark, watery plane.

They grabbed her, pulling with all their might against the horrific strength of the thing in the mirror. For a terrifying second, Mia was stretched between two worlds, the cold of the mirror-world seeping into her bones. With a final, desperate heave, her friends yanked her free.

They scrambled out of the room as the bathroom door slammed shut behind them with a deafening boom that echoed through the school. They ran, their panicked footsteps pounding down the hallway, not daring to look back.

That night, safe in her own bathroom at home, Mia couldn't stop shaking. She avoided looking at her own reflection as she brushed her teeth. But as she leaned in to spit into the sink, she caught a glimpse of her own eyes in the cabinet mirror.

They stared back at her. And for a fraction of a second, one of them slowly, deliberately, winked.

A cold whisper, her own voice but not her own, echoed in the quiet room.

I'm still here.

Chapter 14

The Crawling Inside

Ravenswood school was built on a history of strange disappearances and regurgitated rumours, 17-year-old Clara Bishop felt like she was losing control of her own life. It began as an icy chill that crept beneath her skin each night, a cold that sleep couldn't warm. Then came the voices—soft, sibilant, and almost unintelligible at first—but they soon grew clearer, more insistent, slithering directly into her mind.

"Let me out… let me out, Clara…"
Clara would jolt awake in a cold sweat, her heart hammering against her chest wall. But the horror didn't end with her dreams. During the day, her body became a traitor. Her own hands would twitch, her foot tapping a frantic, uncontrollable rhythm against the floor. Sometimes, her gaze would lock onto things that weren't there—shadows writhing just out of view, gaunt figures standing in the corner of her vision that would vanish when she turned to look.

She tried to ignore it, attributing it to the stress of her A-levels and the general chaos of teenage life. But she soon realised the horrifying truth—

something, or someone, was inside her.

It had all started a few weeks ago when she found an old, cracked mirror hidden behind a loose panel in the school library's forgotten annexe. The mirror was nothing extraordinary, just old and layered with the dust of decades. But when Clara had brushed her fingers against the glass, she'd felt something shift within her, a profound and sickening lurch, as if she had sealed a pact with an unseen entity. She couldn't explain it, but that night, the whispers began.

The voice, pleading at first, soon became a relentless echo in her mind, a demanding presence that crawled into her every thought and movement. It wanted out. And it was getting stronger.
One night, as she sat in her room, the voice came again, sharp and venomous.

"I am trapped, and you will pay for being my cage."

Clara stumbled backwards, knocking over her chair. She looked up at her own bedroom mirror, and her blood ran cold. Her reflection hadn't moved with her. It remained seated, a malevolent grin twisting its features, its eyes hollowed out and black.

Panicking, she searched for answers, turning to her friend, Zoe, a self-proclaimed expert on the supernatural.

"It's a possession," Zoe said, her voice uncharacteristically shaking. "You've touched an object with an attachment, something that was never meant to be found. The spirit is tied to the mirror, but it's latched onto you. It wants freedom, and it will destroy its cage to get out."

Clara felt a growing pressure in her chest, as if the entity was physically pushing against the confines of her skin, desperate to escape. Zoe's warning haunted her: The longer it stays inside you, the more of you it will consume. Clara had no idea how to fight it. Every night, the whispers grew more frantic. "I am you, Clara. You are mine now."

The next day at school, something was different. Clara felt distant, like a passenger in her own body. She moved through the corridors like a puppet, her limbs stiff, her face an expressionless mask. Then, during third period Chemistry, she snapped. Her hands shot out, not of her own volition, and with a surge of unnatural strength, she swept a rack of test tubes from the workbench. They shattered on the floor, acidic contents hissing on the linoleum.

The students stared in shock, but it wasn't Clara looking back at them. It was the ghost, the thing inside her, peering through her eyes with a look of furious triumph. Clara felt a scream building in her own throat, but she was trapped, silenced within her own mind as her body betrayed her.

That night, she stood before her mirror again. The voice was no longer silent—it was a roar that vibrated through her bones.

"You can't stop me. We are one. You will never escape me."

But through the terror clawing at her, Clara realised something. That voice, that rage—it wasn't hers. She had to fight back. She had to reclaim herself.

Zoe's words echoed in her mind: You have to banish it. You're stronger than it thinks you are. In that moment of clarity, Clara slammed her palm against the mirror. The glass spiderwebbed under her touch, and for a brief, haunting moment, the reflection of the ghost stared back, its eyes wild with fury.

"LET ME OUT!" it screamed, the voice now a bitter snarl that ripped from Clara's own throat. But she didn't back down. With every ounce of strength, she focused her will, pushing against the presence, reclaiming her own mind. The mirror began to fracture, groaning under the pressure. And then—silence. The presence inside her vanished.

Clara stumbled back, gasping for air, her breath heavy in her chest. The voice was gone. The suffocating weight had lifted.

She had won.

But as she looked down at the shattered mirror pieces scattered across the floor, she saw something that made her heart stop.

In the largest shard of glass, lying face-up on the floor, her own reflection was staring back up at her. And it was smiling.

Chapter 15

Under The Deep End

Every summer, the kids in the sleepy town of Grey Pines would sneak into the old Birchwood Swim Club—a once-popular country club that had been shut down ten years ago after a string of freak accidents. Nobody really talked about what happened, but rumours swirled around town like leaves in the wind. Some said a girl had drowned and her body was never found. Others claimed a lifeguard had gone mad and cursed the place before vanishing.

Of course, none of that stopped teenagers from making it the go-to dare spot.

One sweltering August night, four friends—Jenna, Marcus, Lila, and Trey—slipped through a gap in the fence with torches, towels, and plan for a little party. The main pool, cracked and full of still, black water, looked more like a wound in the earth now. Algae clung to the sides in thick, green veins. No one in their right mind would swim in it—which is exactly why they were there.

"Whoever jumps in and touches the bottom wins," Trey said, grinning as he stripped to his shorts.

"The bottom?" Jenna asked, eyeing the murky surface. "That thing has to be fifteen feet deep."

"Scared?" Trey teased.

But Marcus, the quiet one, frowned. "I heard no one ever touches the bottom. Like it just keeps going…"

Lila laughed nervously. "That's just a story." They all turned towards the pool. The air around it was still. Too still. Even the crickets had gone quiet. Trey dived first, his body cutting through the water with a heavy splash. The other three watched, their torch beams dancing on the surface, expecting him to resurface.

Ten seconds. Twenty. Thirty.
"Lila," Jenna said, her voice rising in panic. "He's not coming up."

Marcus dropped his torch, which rolled to the edge of the pool, casting a shaky light across the water. Then—a violent splash. Trey burst out of the water, gasping, his eyes wide with terror.

"Something's down there," he panted. "It… it grabbed me."

"You're messing with us," Marcus said, but his voice lacked conviction.

"I swear," Trey snapped, shaking. "It had… fingers."

The group started backing away from the pool

when Lila gave a short scream. Her foot had slipped near the edge. Her torch tumbled in, its light swallowed by the depths in seconds. But as they turned to leave, the water rippled—even though no one was moving.

Then, from the depths, a girl's voice echoed, soft and horribly clear. "Come back… I'm still down here…" All four froze.

"What was that?" Jenna said.
A pale hand shot from the water and yanked Marcus in. He didn't even have time to scream. Trey lunged after him, but the surface snapped shut like a lid, and he was gone too. Lila and Jenna ran, feet pounding the concrete, the voice from the pool chasing them through the dark.

"One more… just one more…"

No one ever found Marcus or Trey. The police drained the pool. It was deeper than they remembered. At the very bottom, in the thick mud, they found a locker key, a girl's bracelet, and something else—a small, childlike skeleton.

The town finally sealed the place off for good. But sometimes, on humid nights, people still claim to hear splashing from behind the fence. And a girl's voice—soft, broken, and eternally lonely:
"Swim with me…"

ONE YEAR LATER

A year had passed, and Grey Pines still whispered their names: Trey Martin. Marcus Delaney. Missing. Presumed dead. But not forgotten. Not by Avery Delaney.

Avery was Marcus's younger sister—seventeen now, sharper than most gave her credit for, and completely convinced her brother wasn't just missing. Something had taken him. Something wrong. And nobody was doing a damn thing about it.

The police? Useless. The town? Terrified into silence. Even Jenna and Lila had vanished—one moved out of state, the other was in a psychiatric hospital. So Avery did what no one else would. She went back to the pool.

Birchwood was under new ownership, rumoured to be turning into a private resort. The grounds were overgrown, patrolled once a week by some half-asleep security guard. The pool was still sealed—drained, chained, and covered with a rusted metal grate.

But it shouldn't have been full.
Avery knelt at the edge, her torch trembling in her hand. The pool gleamed like oil in the moonlight—black, glassy, and full to the brim.

"Still think I imagined it?" Avery asked without

turning.

Behind her, Riley Smith, a local podcaster obsessed with supernatural cold cases, raised an eyebrow. "Nope. Pools don't fill themselves. Especially ones without plumbing."

Riley had been researching the Birchwood case for months. Avery found her online, and the two teamed up. She brought determination. Riley brought gear—and a drive to find the truth that sometimes felt unhinged. They set up cameras and audio recorders around the pool's edge. Everything felt wrong. The air hung heavy. The trees around the courtyard bent inwards, as if listening.

"Why do I feel like we're being watched?" Riley whispered.

Avery didn't answer. Her eyes were locked on the water. Then, it rippled. Just once.

Avery stood up. "I'm going in."
Riley grabbed her arm. "Are you mad?!"

"He's still down there. I can feel it."

"People don't survive underwater for a year, Avery."

"I know," she said, her voice unnervingly calm. "But he's not dead."

Riley stared at her, then slowly let go. "You've got ten minutes. I'm keeping the line tight."

They had brought scuba gear. A full rig. Avery

strapped in, double-checked her harness, and lowered herself into the impossibly cold water.

Below, her torch beam cut through thick, silt-filled darkness. The walls stretched down further than they should. The change was sickeningly organic. Smooth tiles gave way to rough-hewn stone, then to something that felt alive under her gloves—a pulsing, black coral that seemed to breathe. The bottom was gone. In its place was an open void. A tunnel.

Avery's breath quickened. Her gauge read forty feet. Then fifty. Sixty. She should have hit solid ground. Instead, a shape materialised beneath her. Something pale. A face. Eyes stared up—glassy, human. Marcus. He drifted just beyond reach, his lips moving but making no sound.

Avery screamed through her mask and kicked down, hand outstretched. He didn't flee. But then, behind him, something moved. Long, thin fingers stretched from the darkness. A shape with a face like a drowned girl's—eyes black as coal, mouth a hollow smirk. Eliza. She stared at Avery... and smiled.

Dozens more eyes blinked open in the abyss behind her. Painful words flooded Avery's head—in Marcus's voice. In Trey's. In others she didn't know.

"Don't follow me." "It keeps us here." "There's

no surface, Avery." "DON'T LET IT IN."

A sharp pain tore at her ankle. The tether. It went taut. On the surface, Riley screamed and hauled on the rope with all her strength.

Avery exploded out of the water, screaming and thrashing. Riley dragged her onto the concrete and tore off her gear. "What happened?!" she shouted. Avery lay there, eyes wide, gasping. "I saw him. I saw them all. It's not a pool down there… it's a hive, it's a harvest."

Riley paled. "Did you… bring anything up?" Avery froze. On her wetsuit, clinging to her boot, was a strand of black, root-like material. It was wriggling slightly, like it was alive. They both scrambled back.

The water behind them was no longer still. A single, large bubble broke the surface, then another. The black water had begun to boil, and with every bubble that exploded, released the blood and scream of a victim. Hundreds of screams were released. But the final 2, were of Trey and Marcus, their pain echoed out into the silence as one last cry.

A year later the pool was knocked down, and never re-opened again. And everyone just thought their story was a hoax.

Chapter 16

The Last Bell Rings

Jenna wasn't a troublemaker. She was quiet, always on time, and never talked back. So when she got detention for something she didn't do—crude graffiti scrawled in the girls' bathroom—she was more confused than angry. The headteacher's ears were deaf to her pleas, and Mr Fisher, the perpetually grumpy history teacher, simply thrust a slip at her and ordered her to show up Friday at 4 p.m.

The school felt alien after hours. The empty halls swallowed the sound of her footsteps, returning them as distorted echoes. Lockers loomed like cold, steel sentinels, and the flickering dirty lights buzzed overhead like a swarm of dying insects. She made her way to Room 106, a forgotten classroom in the old wing of the building, a place that had been left to rot.

Mr Fisher wasn't there. The door, however, was unlocked. Hesitantly, she stepped inside. The room reeked of must—a cloying mix of wet paper, dust, and something vaguely metallic. The windows were black, starless voids, and the silence pressed in on her, a physical weight on her chest. A single desk lamp at the front of the room sputtered to life. She sat down, telling herself Mr Fisher would be along soon.

Minutes bled into a suffocating half-hour. Still, no one. She stood, a knot of unease tightening in her stomach. Maybe I'm in the wrong room. But as her fingers brushed the doorknob, the door slammed shut with a deafening crack that vibrated through the floor. She recoiled, heart hammering inside her. She tried the handle, it was locked solid.

"Okay… not funny," she said out loud, her voice a thin thread in the oppressive silence.

Then she heard it. The slow, deliberate drag of a heavy desk scraping across the floor. But the sound wasn't from the hallway. It was behind her.

She spun around. All the desks were exactly where they had been. Still. Untouched. Another sound. A faint whisper, seeming to coil right beside her ear. It was her name, but stretched and warped, as if spoken through a broken radio filled with static: "Jeeeennnnaaa…"

Panic seized her. She scrambled backwards toward the window, her breath fogging the glass. Wait. It was a warm evening. Why was it so cold in here? The chalkboard behind the teacher's desk began to screech. White dust rained down as invisible fingers carved a single, sharp word:

DETENTION.

Suddenly, the lights blinked out. Total, suffocating blackness.

Then—footsteps, but not human. They were fast. Skittering. Like the frantic clicks of a cockroach, but heavier. Closer. Jenna fumbled for her phone, its torch a desperate beacon—but the beam died instantly. The battery icon, which had been at 90%, was now a hollow outline. She screamed.

The lights flashed back on for a single, blinding second—just long enough to reveal that all the desks had been violently rearranged into a circle. In the centre stood a lone chair. And in that chair, something sat watching her. It wore a tattered, old-fashioned school uniform, soaked and blackened as if it had been dredged from a muddy river. Its face was hidden beneath a curtain of stringy, wet hair that dripped onto the floorboards.

Its fingers were wrong. Too long. They tapped a slow, hypnotic rhythm on the desk before it. Tap… tap… tap…

The lights went out again.
And Jenna was not alone.

The darkness was a living thing, thick and suffocating. The air grew impossibly cold, and she could hear the faint rustle of wet fabric. Tap… tap… tap. Her mind screamed at her to run, but her feet were rooted to the spot, as if nailed to the floor with rusty jagged nails.

The disturbing footsteps started again, frantic and close. The room seemed to warp around her, the walls stretching and breathing like the inside of a great bloody lung. She glanced at the windows, but they were no longer there. Just solid, impenetrable blackness, as if the world outside had been erased.

The voice returned, a static-laced vibration that rubbed in her bones. "Detention… is forever…"

Jenna spun around. The chair in the centre of the room had moved. She hadn't seen it, hadn't heard it, but it was now directly in front of her. The entity was rising from it.

But then—the door. The one she had tried moments before—it swung open with a low, groaning creak, spilling the dim light of the hallway into the room like a lifeline.

Without a thought, Jenna bolted. Her trembling hand reached for the frame, but just as her fingers were about to cross the threshold, a voice whispered right behind her neck—low, gravelly, and hideously playful: "Leaving so soon?"

She froze. In the doorway, blocking her path, stood a shadow. It was tall and impossibly thin, a towering silhouette with no discernible features. It was a hole in the shape of a man, its outline constantly shifting like smoke.

"Detention," the word echoed, now distorted and layered, a chorus of discordant voices speaking at once. "You never leave…"

Her hand fell from the doorframe. Against her will, she turned to face the room again. The chair was empty.

The skittering started again, but this time from every direction, circling her. More desks slid into view from the shadows, twelve of them, moving on their own, forming a tight, imprisoning circle. In the centre, the figure stood once more. Its face was now visible, and it was a nightmare. A distorted mockery of a teacher, its skin stretched like pale, thin parchment over a broken skull. Its eyes were large sockets, but deep within them, two embers burned with a malevolent light.

It raised a hand, its fingers impossibly long, tapering to sharp points like knives.

"You've been here for a very long time, Jenna," it croaked, its voice the sound of tombstones grinding together. "This is your punishment. You stay… forever…"

The desks pressed in, their edges scraping against her, closing the gap. She was trapped. She opened her mouth to scream, but only a dry rasp escaped.

Everything went black.

When Jenna awoke, she was sitting at a desk. Morning light streamed through the window of Room 106. The other desks were all in their neat, perfect rows.

A nightmare? she thought, her body aching. Her phone was in her hand, the screen glowing. It wasn't dead anymore. She checked the time, and her blood ran cold.

The clock read 4:00 p.m.
The door was locked.

A low, guttural chuckle echoed from the corner of the room. On the chalkboard, a new message was being etched by an unseen hand, the chalk shrieking in protest:

The lesson is about to begin!

Chapter 17

The Vanishing

It happened on a Monday—dreary, grey, and utterly unremarkable. Blackridge School stood at the edge of a quiet town, bordered by thick woods and sickening rumours. The building was old, ivy crawling up its brick walls like haunted features, but it had a strange sense of permanence, as if it had always been there… and always would be.

At 7:55 a.m., students poured into the school as they did every day, shuffling through the gates and yawning down corridors. Teachers sipped lukewarm coffee, and caretakers polished already clean floors. The intercom crackled as the headteacher's voice echoed the same morning greeting. Then, at exactly 8:04 a.m., the bell rang.

And the school vanished.

Not exploded. Not collapsed. Just—gone. The ground where Blackridge school had stood was a perfect, barren square of scorched earth. No rubble. No ash. No smell. Nothing. Just a profound and ringing silence. Cars still sat in the car park, their engines cooling. Backpacks were scattered along the pavement, as if dropped mid-step. Phones inside those bags blinked with unread messages from a world that no longer included their owners.

Emergency crews came. Helicopters circled. The military quarantined the area. Scientists scanned for radiation or seismic activity. Religious leaders prayed. Conspiracy theorists recorded shaky videos about government experiments and portals to hell.

But no one found a single trace of the 463 students and 41 staff who were inside.
Then came the calls.

Parents reported missed video calls from their children at 8:05 a.m.—calls that lasted exactly eleven seconds. All of them. The audio on every recording was the same: ragged breathing, a sound like a distant, howling wind… and scratching. Some claimed to hear their child's voice woven into the static, calling from far away: "Help me." Others heard things they refused to describe, their faces pale with a terror they couldn't voice.

The school was erased from Google Maps within hours. News reports were scrubbed from the internet. Families who pushed for answers were met with sealed lips and cold, dismissive stares. A few who kept digging started disappearing themselves.

A year later, a hiker found something in the woods, miles from where the school once stood: a rusted locker, half-buried in the damp earth, with a single phrase scratched deep into the metal.

STILL HERE.

And every year since, on the anniversary of the disappearance, at 8:04 a.m., phones all over town buzz with a notification: Missed call – Blackridge School.

The town of Blackridge never recovered. People stopped sending their children to other schools and started locking their doors during daylight, whispering about the "curse" that had settled over them. The authorities tried to restore order, but no one trusted them anymore. Not after the way they came in and shut everything down—black vehicles, unmarked helicopters, men in suits who spoke in clipped tones and refused to meet anyone's eye.

Some folks moved away. Most who stayed kept their heads down. But a few… a few demanded answers.

Nina Holland, sister of one of the missing students, started a podcast six months after the vanishing. She called it Dead Ringing. Her brother, Eli, was a junior—top of his class, on the football team, and completely devoted to her. The night before he disappeared, he told her something strange had been happening at school. "There's this door," he'd said over the phone, his voice low. "In the basement. It wasn't there before. No handle. Just… cold. The air around it is freezing."

No one listened to Nina at first. But when she played audio clips from parents, friends, and even a caretaker who survived because he'd called in sick that day—people started tuning in. Then she aired the voicemail.

It was timestamped 8:04 a.m. on the dot. It came from Eli's number, though his phone was never recovered. In the message, there were sounds— scraping metal, a faint school bell, and something like a wet, struggling growl. Then a voice: not Eli's, but one that sounded like dozens of voices speaking at once, a chilling chorus from the void.

It said: "The bell doesn't ring for time. It rings for us."

The podcast exploded. Listeners analysed every second, slowed it down, ran it through filters. One episode had over two million downloads. Then one day, Nina stopped uploading. She had gone back to the site. That was clear from her last text to her producer: "I think it's coming back. I can hear the bell."

Her car was found on the side of the road, engine still running. Her laptop was on the passenger seat, open to an email draft addressed to someone named Mr. Bell. There were no fingerprints on the keyboard.

Every year since, a few people try to reach the

place where Blackridge school once stood. But the woods have grown over the site in a way that feels unnatural—trees too thick, paths that loop back on themselves, time that seems to skip and stutter. Some hikers come back days later, insisting they were only gone for hours.

Some don't come back at all.

Those who do make it close enough say they can hear it. The bell still ringing, calling someone. Calling… you.

And if you ever find yourself near the woods around Blackridge on the third of April at exactly 8:04 a.m.—you might feel your own phone vibrate.

From an unknown number, an uneasy incoming call from something strange and unknown. The question is…

Do you answer?

Chapter 18

Whispers in the Wallpaper

They buried Lila on a Tuesday. A small funeral, grey skies, and more silence than sobs. She was only sixteen. Died in her sleep, the doctor said. No pain. Just a stillness that wouldn't leave.

But Lila woke up anyway. Not in the coffin, not in the cold ground. She woke up in her room, with the faded sunflower wallpaper and the dusty mobile above her bed still spinning gently, as if time hadn't moved. She blinked. Sat up. Everything looked the same. Familiar. Safe. Until she realised no one could see her.

She called out to her mother. Screamed at her father. Pulled at her little brother's arm. Nothing. They walked through her like she was fog. Her mother would stand in the room, staring at the empty bed, whispering Lila's name like a prayer. Her father stayed outside, mending things that didn't need mending. Her brother started talking to the shadows.

Days bled into weeks. Lila began to notice things. The lights in the hallway flickered when she got upset. The wallpaper peeled a little more each time she cried. Sometimes, when her grief was loud enough, the dog would bark at nothing in the corner of the room, hackles raised. She began to understand — she wasn't part of their world anymore. Not fully.

One night, she followed her brother into her old room. He was talking to her—no, to the space where she used to be. "Lila, if you're still here… I miss you," he said to the cold air. She reached for him, her ghostly hand trembling, desperate to touch him just once. In that moment, the clock spun wildly. The wallpaper curled away from the walls like burning paper. Her brother's eyes widened.

He felt her. He never looked at the room the same way again. After that, no one came in. They closed the door. Locked it. The house groaned differently now, as if it were breathing with her. Sometimes they'd hear footsteps when no one was walking. Laughter that didn't belong to anyone alive. Her mother started sleeping with the lights on.

Lila stopped trying to be seen. But the house remembered her. And every child that moved into that room after, every girl who slept beneath the sunflower wallpaper, would whisper the same thing to their parents: "There's a girl here. She watches me sleep."

No one believed them. But Lila never left. She just waited—quiet, unseen—for someone to finally notice.

Years passed. Families came and went, but Lila's room always stayed strangely untouched. The wallpaper, faded and brittle, was never replaced. No one could stand to be in there long enough. They said it felt wrong. Cold, even in summer. The floorboards creaked when no one was there. The eyes of dolls would shift ever so slightly when you weren't looking.

The girl who finally saw Lila was named Gemma. She was eight. Quiet. A little strange, her parents said. Always talking to things that weren't there. They moved into the house in October.

The first night, Gemma walked straight into Lila's room—her room—and stood in the middle of it as if listening to something no one else could hear. Then she smiled. "I know you're here," she said to the empty air.

Lila froze. She hadn't been truly seen in years. Not since her brother. Not really. Sophie turned, her eyes wide and knowing. "You're lonely."

Lila drifted closer, uncertain. Hopeful. Gemma began to talk to her every night. Not just to the air—to her. She told her stories, drew her pictures, even left toys where Lila's ghostly hands could just barely brush against them. The room grew warmer. Less hateful. Lila's restless presence softened. The lights flickered less.

But with every passing day, Gemma changed. Her eyes grew darker. She stopped speaking to her parents, saving all her words for the silent room. Her drawings turned eerie—pictures of a pale girl with lifeless eyes, of wallpaper that looked like it was bleeding, of a door with no handle. Then one morning, Gemma didn't wake up.

The doctors said it was her heart. Quiet, like Lila's. Peaceful. But her parents knew something was wrong. The room felt heavier than grief. It felt like something had rooted itself deep in the wood and plaster, and it wouldn't let go.

That night, a clock spun again. And in the silence of the house, if you were listening closely, you could hear two little girls laughing—softly, from behind the locked door.

Lila wasn't alone anymore. And no one else would ever sleep in that room again.

At least for now.

Chapter 19

Porcelain Voices

No one really noticed when Kayla started acting differently. At first, it was subtle—missing homework, staring off during class, smiling when nothing was funny. But things got weirder, and fast.

It all started after she found the doll. It was hidden in a dusty cardboard box in her grandmother's attic after she became ill—a porcelain-faced doll with pale blue eyes and a tiny, cracked smile. Her grandmother said it was hers when she was a girl, but her expression tightened when she spoke of it. "Just keep it in the box," she warned, her voice thin. "She doesn't like being out for too long."

But Kayla didn't listen. She brought it home, cleaned the grime from its painted face, and set it on the shelf in her room.

That night, she heard a quiet voice. Soft at first, like static. Then clearer, luring her in "You're not like the others, Kayla. You listen." The next day, she wore her school uniform backwards. When people laughed, she just smiled, her eyes unsettlingly blank.

The voice grew louder. Soon, she was locking herself in toilet cubicles, singing strange, discordant lullabies. She started scrawling symbols on the chalkboard before class began. Teachers scolded her—until one of them vanished without a trace. After that, no one said a word.

Her best friend, Zoe, tried to confront her. "Kayla, this isn't you. What's going on?" she asked during lunch, her voice trembling. Kayla looked up, but the voice that answered wasn't quite her own. "She says you don't believe. That's dangerous."

That night, Zoe's house burned down. The official cause was faulty wiring, but Kayla's smile stretched wider the next morning, excited at the fear they experienced.

Finally, someone noticed the doll. A teacher saw her talking to it in her locker. Her eyes were glassy, her mouth trembling, as if she were receiving orders. When he tried to take it, he collapsed on the floor, seizing violently. Kayla just stood there. Watching and smiling.

They expelled her after that and she went missing, but she never truly left. Sometimes, students say they still hear her singing in the empty halls and rocker rooms. And on stormy nights, the caretaker swears he sees a small porcelain doll sitting on Kayla's old desk, waiting. Eyes wide and head twisting.

If you find it—don't listen. Because once she

speaks to you, she never lets go and you become her new obsession.

Zoe did survive the fire, she woke up in hospital with angry red burns on her arms and smoke still stinging her lungs. The investigators ruled it an accident. But Zoe remembered the sounds just before the flames erupted—the creak of porcelain, a soft, high-pitched giggle, and a screech that didn't belong in her head: "She told you to believe."

No one believed her. Not the doctors. Not her parents. But she knew it wasn't over.

Back at school, Kayla was gone—but not forgotten. Her desk sat empty, the chair never moved. Students avoided that corner of the classroom at all costs. A heavy silence still hung there, thick, haunting and cold.

Then Zoe started seeing her. In mirrors. First in the girls' toilets—the reflection of a girl in a skirt too long for her body, her smile a thin, porcelain crack. Then in the glass doors of the library, in the shimmer of car windows as she walked home. Kayla, just staring. The doll held loosely in her hands.

Zoe tried to ignore it, but the voices clawed for her at night. Only this time, they felt like they were coming from inside her own head. She'd wake up standing beside her window, the glass cold beneath her fingertips. Or find strange words scrawled on her bedroom wall, the handwriting spidery and unfamiliar. Her hands moved on their own sometimes, as if pulled by invisible strings.

One morning, she opened her school bag and found the doll inside. Its head was tilted at a slightly different angle. Its painted lips seemed parted now. And it whispered, clear as day: "She chose you next."

Zoe threw it into the river behind the school that night. She watched it sink into the dark, murky water, its pale skin vanishing beneath the current. But it came back. It was sitting on her desk the next morning. Perfectly dry. Smiling.

Zoe stopped sleeping. She delved into old newspapers, school records, local legends. One night, deep in news archives, she found it: a faded article from 1953. A girl named Ellen Wren, expelled from the very same school. Accused of witchcraft after students vanished and teachers were driven mad. The mystery ended when the school burned down in an unexplained fire. Ellen's body was never found.

But something else was. A porcelain doll, pulled from the ashes. The description was exact—blue eyes, pale skin, the same cracked smile. The article ended with a quote from the old headmaster: "She doesn't possess the doll. She is the doll."

The pieces clicked into place in Zoe's mind. Ellen had somehow transferred her soul into the porcelain. Waiting. Feeding on belief, on fear. Each girl she "chose" became a puppet—a vessel she could wear for a while before hollowing them out completely. Kayla was just the latest skin. Zoe was meant to be the next.

But Zoe had something the others didn't—she wasn't afraid anymore. She was furious and needed to be free.

She went back to Kayla's grandmother's and broke in, she climbed into the attic, the place it was first freed. There, beneath the roof floorboards, Zoe found an old iron box. It was inscribed with strange words and sealed with wax. Zoe also found an old news article, the grandmother had been one of the survivors of the first fire, she knew that Ellen's soul had been trapped. But now Zoe knew what she had to do, she had to get rid of this curse for good.

That night, as the torment in her head grew into screams and the doll crawled into her bed on its own—its porcelain limbs twitching unnaturally—Zoe lit the candles, drew the sigil on the floor, and read the incantation aloud. The doll screamed. Not a sound in the room, but a deafening wail of hatred and hunger inside her mind.

Then, silence. The doll slumped over, its eyes wide but finally lifeless.

Zoe locked it in the iron box and sealed it shut. She buried it six feet deep under salted earth, far from the school.

But last week, a first-year girl at the school unexpectedly found something in her locker. It was a small porcelain doll. Still with a cracked smile and sinister look within its eyes.

And somewhere, deep beneath the ground, Zoe felt a crack form in her dreams—a single voice, breaking through the silence: "You can't bury me forever."

The next night, Zoe woke up suddenly, she was trapped in an iron box, buried six feet deep under the earth, with no escape. Something sharp and jagged was poking into her back and all the way down her body. She couldn't see, but it felt like she was laying on the bones of another, taken before her, likely Kayla.

She screamed and clawed at the box, breaking off some nails. But it was no use, she was trapped and no one knew where she was. All she could do now is panic and await the same ending as Kayla, a slow suffocating and frightening death.

Chapter 20

The Devil's Threshold

It started as a dare. Three teen friends—Maya, Jace, and Eliza—spent their last summer night exploring the woods behind Eliza's grandfathers's old farmhouse. It was humid and the heavy buzz of insects.

Beneath the roots of a worn down oak, Jace stumbled on something odd: a rusted iron latch, half-buried in the soil. Curious, they dug around it. It was a trapdoor.

The wooden planks groaned as they prised it open. A narrow stone staircase descended into absolute blackness. The strong smell of burnt ash rushed up to meet them. "This is insane," Maya said, already filming on her phone. "Let's check it out."

At the bottom, they found a small, circular chamber—walls lined with melted candles, scorched animal bones, and a thick, leather-bound book resting on a pedestal carved from black stone.

"Eliza, was your gramps into… weird stuff?" Jace asked, half-joking. Eliza shook her head. "He never mentioned anything like this." The book was heavy. Bound in something disturbingly like skin, it seemed to come alive when they opened it. Not in a metaphorical way—actual voices, low and hissing, crept out from the ancient pages. Latin words, twisted symbols, and diagrams of something clawed and burning filled the parchment.

"It says we can open a gate," Maya said, her voice barely audible. "Just for a moment. To… see."

Jace grinned, his bravado masking his fear. "Let's do it."

They lit the candles and recited the incantation from the first page. The floor shuddered. The pedestal cracked, splitting open like a dry mouth, and from it bled shadows and distant screams. The stone beneath their feet peeled away, revealing a chasm—red and endless—filled with indistinct things. Panic really set in when the air turned to sulphur.

"Guys," Eliza said, backing away, "we need to stop—"

But something reached up from the pit. Long, black fingers wrapped around Jace's ankle. His scream was the last thing they heard before he was yanked down hard, hitting his head with a loud crack and vanishing into the abyss.

Maya lunged, but the hole sealed shut as if it had never been there. Then the candles blew out. The book snapped closed, and the room was silent again.

Except for a voice. It came from the pages, a sibilant tone in the dark. "One has been claimed. Two more to go."

Maya dropped the book as if it were on fire. Eliza started sobbing. They ran and climbed out as quickly as they could.

They never told anyone what happened, they were too scared, they played dumb and said they were not with him that day. Jace's body was never found and he was classed as a missing person.

But every night, the book reappeared at one of their homes—on a bed, in the fridge, reflected in a mirror. And each time, a new page was open, a new message scrawled in what looked like blood: NEXT.

Maya hadn't slept in days. After the night Jace was taken, she'd burned the spell book in Eliza's back garden. She watched the flames swallow the leather cover, listened as it shrieked while the pages curled and blackened. She thought that would be the end of it.

But the next morning, it was on her nightstand. Open to a new page. Her name was written across the top in something red, thick, and wet. MAYA – THE EYE IS UPON YOU, YOU'RE NEXT.

She didn't tell Eliza. What could she say? That a cursed book was stalking her? That she heard screams at night, smelled ash in her dreams, and saw Jace—twisted and broken—behind her eyes every time she blinked?

But also she couldn't hide it for long. Especially after she found the mark. It was just above her hip, etched into her skin like a brand—an eye with three slashes through it. It pulsed beneath her skin. Hot, it felt alive. When she showed Eliza, her friend's face went white.

"I have one too," she said, lifting the back of her shirt. The same mark was carved between her shoulder blades deep into her skin.

They decided to return to the woods that night, back to the trapdoor to burn it down—except it was gone. The ground was solid, with no sign it had ever been there. But the air still smelled of sulphur. That's when the voices came again. From the trees this time. From the earth. From their own mouths. "Two more to go."

Eliza clutched Maya's hand. "We need help. Someone who knows about this."

"There is someone," Maya said, her voice shaking. "My aunt. She used to be into… occult stuff. Banishing rituals, demon lore. I thought she was nuts."

They traveled two hours to find her. Aunt Beth lived in a cabin, deep in the hills, off-grid and alone. When she saw the marks, her face hardened.

"I told your mother this would happen," she muttered. "You kids always think these things are games. That book? It's a Threshold Grimoire. There are only three copies in existence. And they don't disappear—they attach. Once you read from it, it's yours. It watches you. It marks you. It wants three souls."

"Then how do we stop it?" Maya pleaded. "How do we get Jace back?"

Beth's eyes narrowed. "You don't get him back. But you might save yourselves." She pulled out a dagger—cold iron, etched with symbols—and a vial of black salt. "You'll need to return to the gate. Reopen it. And offer it something else."
"Something else?" Eliza asked, her voice a thin thread.

Beths's voice was grim. "A soul. Willing or not." A knock echoed from the front door. Three times. Loud. Imperative.

Beth didn't move. "Don't answer that," she said quietly. The knock came again. Louder. Then the door began to burn. From the inside out. And the book was there again, sitting on the floor between them. Open to a new page.

CHOOSE.

The room fell into an eerie silence. The figure—the shadow in the doorway—moved closer, its burning eyes locked onto Maya with an almost mocking intensity. It was waiting.

Maya's breath hitched. She could feel Eliza's gaze on her, feel her friend's hand trembling in hers. "Maya, please… don't do this," Eliza begged. "Don't let it take me."

"A soul must be willing," Beths's words echoed in Maya's head. "The sacrifice must be made by choice, or the gate will claim all of you."

The truth hit her like a physical blow. The book didn't just want a soul; it wanted a choice. A betrayal. It wanted one of them to condemn the other. If she refused, they would both be lost.

A terrible, cold clarity settled over her. There was only one way.

"I'm sorry," Maya shouted, her voice thick with a grief that was already consuming her. She turned, not to Eliza, but to the shadow in the doorway. She let go of Eliza's hand.

"I choose," Maya said, her voice clear and steady now. "I offer a soul."

The figure tilted its head. The burning in its eyes intensified. "I choose me."

For a moment, nothing happened. The air crackled with tension. Eliza stared, her eyes wide with disbelief and dawning horror. "No… Maya, no!"

The shadow let out a sound that was not a laugh, but the grating of bent metal on stone. "A worthy sacrifice," the voice hissed in her mind. "But the price for one soul is another's freedom. Is she worth it?"

The book on the floor flipped to its final page. New words bled into the parchment. THE PACT IS SEALED.

Then, the mark on Eliza's back flared with an unbearable heat, and she screamed as it burned away, leaving her skin clean. The brand on Maya's hip, however, turned black and began to spread, dark veins crawling up her skin like ink seeping through tissue paper.

"Maya!" Eliza cried, reaching for her. But Maya was already changing. Her skin grew pale and translucent, her eyes sinking into dark, hollow caves. She looked at her friend, a single tear tracing a path down her cheek. "Run," she rasped, her voice already becoming a dry, rattling echo.

The shadow figure dissolved, melting into Maya, pouring into her mouth and eyes until she was no longer a girl, but a silhouette of painful darkness herself. The book slammed shut. The fire on the door went out.

The room was still. Aunt Beth was gone too. The only things left were Eliza, sobbing on the floor, and the thing that had taken Maya, standing where the doorway had been. It was now the next guardian. The new gatekeeper, ready for the next sacrifice.

And it was smiling.

Chapter 21

The Thing That Calls

At Hookpine Secondary School, there was a rule between the students that nobody ever broke: never open your window after midnight. Everyone knew the story. Or at least, a version of it.

The first disappearance was Lauren Mays. A straight-A student, captain of the athletics team, and probably the last person anyone thought would just vanish. She went to bed like any other night. The next morning, her parents found her room empty—the bed still made, her phone still charging, her shoes placed neatly on the floor. And her window? Wide open.

There was no sign of a struggle. No prints. No scent trail for the dogs. Just the icy wind crawling in from the woods behind the house and a strange pattern of scratches on the windowsill. Long. Deep. As though something with claws had prised it open.

For weeks, the police searched. Nothing. No leads. No sightings. Just a profound and unnerving emptiness. Until it happened again. And again. Each time, the same pattern: a teenager disappearing from their bedroom in the dead of night, always with their window open, shoes on the floor, and no signs of forced entry. That's when the stories really started and things became too weird. They called it The Caller.

No one could remember who came up with the name. It just… spread. Like a bad rumour with a heartbeat. The older students talked about it in hushed voices, the way you talk about something that might be real but is definitely not safe.

They said it was tall—unnaturally so. Thin as a corpse left out in the woods. It moved like smoke and shadows, slipping through cracks in walls and the seams of your dreams. Its face was wrong and evil. Blurred, scared and unfinished. Some said it wore the faces of people you loved. Others claimed it didn't have a face at all, just a black void and a voice like dripping water in a deep, dark well. But everyone agreed on one thing: It called to you.

From just outside your window, it teased your name. Sweet and almost tender. It knew what you feared and what you longed for. It promised comfort, escape and belonging. It made you feel seen, wanted, and needed. And then it took you.

Some believed it didn't kill you straight away; that it needed to possess you first, breaking you down from the inside. Others said it lured you into the forest and fed on you slowly, keeping you alive just long enough to feel every moment of it. But no one ever came back to tell the truth.

Lena Harlow was a quiet, observant teen who mostly kept to herself. She'd heard the stories, of course. Everyone had. But she didn't believe in monsters. She believed in sleepwalking, teenage runaways, and collective hysteria. Until the night she heard it.

It was just past 2 a.m. The wind had picked up, rustling the trees outside her room. She was lying in bed, half-asleep, when she heard something—soft, delicate, and impossibly close. "Lena…"

She sat bolt upright, her heart thudding with blood. At first, she thought it was her mum. But the voice was wrong, it was too low and too smooth. It sounded like it was sliding under her skin. She got out of bed and approached the window slowly. The glass was fogged with her breath. But there, just beyond it—she saw a figure. Thin. Lank. Its limbs too long, too crooked. It was standing impossibly still in the middle of the garden, its head tilted at an unnatural angle. Then it moved, and not like a human.

It didn't walk—it slid. Closer. Closer. She stumbled back just as a whisper pressed against the glass, seeming to vibrate through it. "You don't have to be alone anymore, Lena… Let me inside you."

She screamed. Her parents burst into the room

seconds later, but when they looked outside, there was nothing. Just the wind and the trees. But Lena knew. It had been real.

After that, things changed. Lena stopped sleeping. Every night, she heard it—calling her name, telling her it understood, that it could make everything better for her. She tried to tell people. Her parents sent her to a therapist. Her friends eventually pulled away. Even the teachers started to look at her with wary eyes. It wanted her isolated. Vulnerable.

One night, she found herself standing by the window with her hand on the latch, not even remembering how she got there. She slammed it shut and backed away, sobbing. The next day, she learned that Jenny Lin was gone. Jenny, her lab partner. The only one who still talked to her. Her window had been open. Shoes on the floor.

Desperate, Lena broke into the local press office and searched the news archives. Buried in old manuscripts and town records, she found something chilling. Hookpine had always been quiet. But every twenty years, like clockwork, there had been disappearances. Always teenagers, always at night. Always with open windows. Folklore from the area told of an old creature from before the town was founded—something that fed on youth, loneliness, and fear. Something that mimicked love to lure the lost. It had many names. The Hollow. The Hunger. The Caller. But no one really knew.

It wasn't a ghost. It wasn't a man. It was ancient. And it was hungry again.

Lena made a choice. She couldn't run. She wouldn't let it take anyone else. So she waited. She set up her phone to record. She left the window unlatched. And when the whisper came, she opened it.

"I knew you'd come," it said, its voice a sickening caress as it stepped forward, impossibly tall, grinning with teeth like black needles and knives for fingers.

Lena didn't back away. She stood firm. "You're not real," she said, her voice shaking but defiant.

It laughed, a sound like dry leaves skittering across pavement. "Neither is your loneliness," it whispered back. "But you believe in that, don't you?"

It reached for her. And that's when she struck the match.

The creature screamed as the line of salt and alcohol she'd poured around her bed caught fire, a sudden, violent burst of white light tearing through the room. It howled and staggered back, its skin blistering, its form unravelling into smoke and scorched bone. And just like that—it was gone.

Lena didn't remember falling asleep, but when she woke, the sun was rising, and the window was closed and locked. She showed the footage to her parents. The school. The police. But the video file was corrupted. Just static. They said she'd had a psychotic episode. That it was grief, stress, trauma.

But Lena knew. The Caller was real. It was just waiting again, sleeping off its wounds.
And next time, it would call for someone else, ready to stroke and glide its knife like fingers through their hair

Maybe… you.

Chapter 22

The Curse of Langley School

They always said something was wrong with Langley School. The rumours started small like they normally do: odd smells in the corridors, lights turning off during class, cold spots in the middle of summer. But that all changed the day of the blood moon.

It began with a girl named Marcy. One day she collapsed in the canteen, convulsing, screaming that something was inside her. When the teachers pulled her away, her mouth was full of black bile—and her last words before her eyes rolled back were, "He's awake now." By the end of the week, six more students had gone missing, the authorities started closing everything down whilst a manhunt was on.

The curse spread like a virus though. One by one, students would show the signs: broken blood vessels in their eyes, voices from within their lockers, bones creaking as if trying to escape their own skin. Then came the hunger. Not their own hunger—but something else's.

It was the demon: Vorrak, a parasite bound to the school since the 1800s, when the land it was built on was used for occult rituals. A cult had tried to summon eternal knowledge. Instead, they got him—a demon who feeds by hollowing out souls from the inside, eating fear, pain, and flesh alike. And now, he was free again. So the myth goes, but no one was really sure, but we were all trying to find answers.

The curse passed like an infection. If you locked eyes with someone already "marked," Vorrak would jump. You'd feel a scratch in your gut, like claws dragging along your spine. Then you'd start to rot— slowly, from the inside out. And the worst part? You'd feel every second of it. You would scream, but only in your head. Your body wouldn't be yours anymore.

Teachers tried to cover it up. The headteacher was the first to be consumed. By the time the town figured out what was happening, the school's corridors were a maze of black veins and ash, and the students were either possessed—or pieces of rotten meat.

Only one survived: Danny Miro. No one knows why. He just walked out of the burning school the next morning, covered in soot and blood, repeating one word: "Run."

Over time they rebuilt Langley school, some still say on a full moon, after hours you can hear the words being chanted around the halls "He's hungry again."

Danny, a little older was sat at his desk in first period, pretending to pay attention to the teacher droning on about history, but Marcy's face kept replaying in his mind. The panic in her eyes, the way she'd screamed about something inside her. He couldn't shake the feeling her last words were meant for him.

He skipped lunch and hid in the fitness hall, but the echoed silence didn't help. By his last class, the unease had curdled into a cold, creeping dread. The school buzzed with nervous energy, but it was the quiet that bothered him. No one was shouting or laughing. Everyone's eyes were just… blank. As though they'd all been muted.

That's when he saw Ben Kline walking across the hall. Ben had always been the class clown. Now, his face was pale, his hands shaking, his eyes darting around as if he were seeing things no one else could. Ben stopped right in front of Danny. His chest heaved.

"Get away from me." Ben's voice cracked. He grabbed Danny by the collar, his fingers like ice. "You… you've seen it, haven't you?"

"I don't know what you're talking about," Danny said, trying to pull away.

"It's inside me," Ben choked out, his eyes wild. "I

saw it. It's crawling, Danny. It's crawling inside me!"

The tremor in Ben's hands became a full-blown convulsion. He opened his mouth to scream, but no sound came out. Instead, black blood began to leak from the corners of his eyes. Before Danny could react, Ben's body collapsed with a sickening thud, it was like his skin fell off his bones.

The hall seemed to stretch on forever. Other students gathered, but no one screamed. No one even moved. They just stared at Ben's body as if it wasn't there. And then… they all looked at Danny. All at once. Their eyes locked on him. Blank. Empty. Unblinking.

His heart stopped. He tried to look away, but it was too late. He felt it. A scratch. Under his ribs. Sharp and insistent. His vision blurred. The torment started in his mind, picking at him. It's in me, too.

He staggered backwards, his hand bracing against the wall. His fingertips left a smear of blood on the cold brick, his own blood. The whispers grew louder, but this time, they were no longer just in his head. A sound, soft but unmistakable, slithered from the empty, bloodshot eyes of the students watching him. They weren't looking at him anymore. They were waiting. Waiting for him to fall. Danny ran out of the hall screaming, trying to run away from the fear and for the pan to go away. He knew it was coming for him, it was just a matter of time.

That night, Danny couldn't sleep. Every time he closed his eyes, he saw those blank faces. The cold crawl under his skin never stopped, slicing at his finger tips. He was terrified to fall asleep—terrified he'd wake up and no longer be himself. He searched online for anything that could explain what was happening. One story caught his eye: The Demon of Langley: A History of the Curse.

It was about a ritual performed when the school was first built, meant to bind a demon named Vorrak to the land. The curse had been sealed, the article said, but something had broken that seal. Something had woken it up. And now, it was hunting again. He couldn't finish reading. He couldn't breathe, he was to scared.

By morning, the scratch had become a deep, throbbing burn. He stood before the mirror, eyes sunken. When he opened his mouth, he saw something moving in the back of his throat. Something black and twitching.

At school, there were more empty desks. The students who remained weren't normal. He saw it in their eyes. Too wide. Too still. One kid in biology was chewing his pencil—wood and all—and didn't even flinch when it cracked his tooth.

Mr Kemple, his history teacher, stopped him in the corridor. "You've got the mark," he said, his own face pale and sweating.

"Who is he? What is this?" Danny grabbed his arm.

Mr Kemple leaned in close. "He's called Vorrak. A demon older than the bones of the earth. The school's built on a gate—something the founders thought they sealed. But the rituals woke him. And once he's awake, he feeds."

The burn behind Danny's ribs flared. For a moment, he swore he could hear breathing. From inside him. "Then how do I stop it?"

Mr Kemple stared at him. "You don't," he said, his voice a ghost of a shadow. "You burn it all down, we burn it all down."

By sundown, the school was a graveyard. Students sat silent in class, staring forward with mouths slightly open. Teachers moved like puppets. The walls had started to pulse—faint, flesh-coloured veins running just beneath the paint. The thing inside Danny was hungry now. It spoke in his own voice, telling him to give in, that the pain would stop if he just let it take over.

He ran to the boiler room. Mr Kemple was already there, hands trembling, holding a canister of petrol. "We only get one shot," he said. "Once the fire starts, he'll try to escape. Into you. Into anything still alive."

Danny looked down at his arms. His veins were blackening beneath the skin. His fingernails had turned sharp, almost like claws. "It's already too late for me," he said.

Mr Kemple hesitated. "Not if you're stronger than it is."

Danny poured the petrol. The flames caught fast—too fast. The building groaned, the walls rippling like living skin. Screams echoed through the halls—but they weren't human. They were inside him. They festered quickly within his body, stretching his insides.

Then came the final choice for Danny as Mr Kemple was burned alive. The fire climbed the walls, smoke filled his lungs, and the demon inside him howled for release. Danny turned, not towards the exit though, but towards the heart of the inferno instead.

He felt a moment of peace as the painful flames met his skin. He knew this was time to stop tis misery once and for all, for everyone. He leapt into the flames.

And as the building collapsed, he made sure the demon burned with him, forever.

Chapter 23

Tomorrow's Eyes

Sixteen-year-old Ava Hart always knew she was different. While her friends worried about crushes and fashion, Ava struggled with visions—terrifying flashes of the future that came without warning and left her breathless. Sometimes they were harmless: a broken glass, a friend's scraped knee. But lately… they'd turned dark.

It started one rainy Thursday night. Ava woke up at 3:07 a.m., heart beating loud, cold sweat soaking her sheets. In her dream, she'd seen a girl—her face bloodied, her mouth open in a scream that made no sound. Behind her, a shadow moved, something long and thin in its hand. Ava didn't recognise the girl… until the next morning, when she passed her in the school corridor. Her name was Jessica—a new transfer student. She had the same nervous smile, the same silver locket.

Ava tried to ignore it. A coincidence. But the next night brought another vision: Jessica, crying in the school toilets, her hands stained red. And then, the worst one yet—Jessica lying motionless in the woods behind the school, eyes wide open, staring directly at Ava.

Panicked, Ava tried to warn her. She approached Jessica at lunch, her voice shaking. "Do you ever walk home through the woods? Just… don't. Please."

Jessica gave her a weird look and laughed it off. "You're kind of intense, you know that?"

The following Friday, Jessica didn't show up for school.

That night, Ava had another vision—but this time, she wasn't just watching. She was in the woods, holding a torch, her breath fogging in the air. She stumbled over roots until the beam caught something pale. A hand.

She jolted awake. She had never tested the visions before. They always came true—unless she changed something. She had to try. She ran into the woods, rain pouring, the trees looming over her like giants.

And then—movement. She found Jessica, barely conscious, a gash across her forehead. "She tried to kill me," she stated. "I ran. I think she's still—"

A twig snapped. Ava turned just in time to see a figure step out of the darkness. A woman. A teacher. Miss Jones, the one who always stayed late to "help students." She smiled when he saw her. "I was hoping you'd come," she said.

But Ava was ready. She'd seen this moment. And

n this vision, she survived.

Miss Jones lunged at her. But Ava had seen this—every step, every breath, the exact angle of her attack. She ducked, grabbed the rusted torch, and slammed it into her knee. She howled. Jessica screamed too, they both ran. Branches clawed at their faces cutting them. The rain blurred everything and mixed with blood and sweat. But Ava could still see. Not with her eyes—but with the future. Her mind flashed images like a broken film reel: the left fork leads to a dead end. The right path—freedom. They veered right, not stopping until they burst out onto the road, collapsing in front of a passing car.

Miss Jones was arrested. It turned out Jessica wasn't the first. The news called Ava a quiet hero. But her visions didn't stop. In fact, they came more often now—sharper, clearer… and colder. She started seeing strangers. A little boy trapped in a sinking car. A man stepping into a lift that would never reach the ground floor. It was like the world had cracked open, and every horror hidden in the shadows was being fed straight into her brain.

Worst of all, she started seeing herself. Dying. Over and over. But the same person was always there, just out of focus. A silhouette. Watching. Waiting for her.

One night, the visions suddenly stopped, there was a peaceful silence. For the first time in months, Ava felt normal. Until she got a text from an unknown number: "You saw me. Didn't you?" The attachment showed a screenshot from her own nightmare. Ava. On the floor. Lifeless. And in the background—blurry but unmistakable—the shadow watching her again. Only now, it was closer to her.

She threw the phone across the room, but the image stayed, burned into her mind. The next morning, everything felt… off. The air was too still. People at school avoided her eyes.

That night, she woke up standing outside. Barefoot on the cold, wet grass. And in the field behind her house—it was waiting. The shadow. Same shape, same silence, but now it had eyes. Eyes like broken mirrors, reflecting a thousand dying stars. It lifted a hand—slow, deliberate—and pointed directly at her. Then, it communicated. Not in words, but in visions. Hundreds of them, flashing all at once. Futures. Deaths. Catastrophes. Ava falling through ice. Ava tied to a chair. A fire. A face. Her own grave.

And then—one vision that felt different. Her, older. Stronger. Standing in a circle of mirrors. Blood on her hands. The shadow behind her—but this time, she wasn't afraid. She was smiling.

She woke up gasping. It took days to understand. The visions twisted, turned cruel. They no longer showed the truth. They lied. She tried saving a boy from a bike accident—he broke his arm because she startled him. The future was splintering. She wasn't seeing what would happen anymore. She was seeing what someone wanted her to see.

Her gift wasn't hers alone. Someone—or something—was inside her visions now. Twisting them. Feeding her fear. Bending her into exactly what it wanted her to become. The final message came three weeks later. Not a photo. Not a warning. Just three words: "Ready to trade?"

Ava didn't understand. Until she saw Jessica again. Only this time, Jessica had visions too. But hers were different. Clearer. Darker. Something had passed between them that night in the woods. A tether. A trade. The future was no longer a window. It was a weapon. And Ava was learning how to use it.

She stopped fighting the visions and started listening. When she let go of fear, the flashes became clearer, sharper. The screaming stopped. The images obeyed. She was no longer just watching the future. She was shaping it. It started small. She guided a lost girl away from a stranger's van. Made her cheating ex trip in front of the whole school. Little things. But it felt good. It was incredibly powerful.

Then came the night she dreamt of the fire again. This time, she set it. A scorched house, with a man inside. One of Miss Jones old friends— someone who "didn't know anything." But Ava's visions said otherwise. The next morning, the house was ashes. And in her inbox was a new message: "Good. You're learning." The Watcher was still with her. But now… it felt like a mentor.

Meanwhile, Jessica's visions were clean. Precise. She could see patterns, days ahead. She used hers for good, predicting a gas leak and saving an entire apartment building. Until one day, she showed up at Ava's door, pale and shaking. "I saw you," she said.

"You're not just seeing the future. You're making it. I saw you in a hospital, hooked up to machines. They were trying to stop your brain from burning itself alive." Ava tilted her head. "Was I scared?"

Jessica shook her head. "No. You were smiling." The Watcher had a name.

The visions dragged Ava to an old, abandoned mental hospital. Where Dr Elias Wren, psychic researcher disappeared in 1982. He was obsessed with "chronoperception"—bending time through thought. He had patients. Young girls who were gifted. Most didn't survive his experiments. His final notes were scrawled in red ink: "The girl isn't seeing the future. The future is seeing her. And it wants her back."

Ava ran her fingers across the writing and felt something behind her. She turned—and saw herself. She was older and lifeless Wearing the same smile from the visions and eyes like mirrors. The Watcher wasn't Elias. It was Ava. A version of her that lost control, that surrendered to the visions so completely that time bent around her like glass. Every voice, every message, every manipulated dream—was always her own voice. Calling back. Teaching her. Becoming her completely.

Jessica is the only one who can stop it now. But Ava isn't sure she wants to be saved anymore. For the first time in her life… she's the one writing the future.

The visions had stopped for Jessica though. Not because she'd lost them—because Ava had taken them. Every path Jessica tried to follow, Ava had already walked. Every future she tried to change had been rewritten. Ava had become something else now. Not fully human. Her eyes shimmered with the silver light. Her presence made clocks glitch. Her voice sometimes echoed before her lips moved. She had become unstuck in time—and she liked it.

Jessica made one last plan. One final, flickering

vision. A sliver of a possibility where Ava stopped herself. It could only happen in one place: The Mirror Room, deep beneath the ruins of Dr Wren's hospital. A circle of twelve cracked, ancient mirrors, each showing a different Ava. One was kind. One was monstrous. One was dead. And one… one was still human.

Jessica waited until midnight. Rain was falling through holes in the ceiling. The mirrors pulsed softly, as if breathing. And waiting too

Then Ava stepped in, she knew her calling. No footsteps, just presence. Her voice was calm, distant. "I warned you not to follow me."

"You're still in there," Jessica said. "You sent yourself back. You tried to save yourself."
Ava glanced at the mirrors. "That was a different me."

"No," Jessica insisted. "It was you before this took everything."

A long silence. Then Ava raised her hand—and the mirrors shattered. But not into shards. Into visions. Each broken piece hovered, glowing, playing a different future. A thousand ways the world could end. Or be saved. Ava stepped into the swirl of them, laughing softly. "You don't get it, Jess. I'm not seeing time anymore." She paused. "I am time."

Jessica reached into her pocket. A mirror shard. From a version of Ava who had died trying to stop this loop. The one who failed—but left a piece of herself behind. Jessica pressed it into Ava's chest. And everything stopped.

Ava slowly opened her eyes. She was sixteen, but felt different. Back in her room. Rain tapping against the window. Her phone buzzed. She looked down to a message. "You saw me. Didn't you?"

But this time, she didn't delete it. She stared at it. And spoke only, "Not again."

Because deep inside her—beneath the fear, beneath the visions—was the memory of what she became. The Watcher. The Monster. The girl who tried to own time and lost herself to it. Now, she had a choice. The loop was broken.

But the future was still hers to write, and she had the power to see all futures.

Chapter 24

The Ashen Curse

It was supposed to be just another harmless thrill. Eli and Jordan, both seventeen and hungry for a rush, had heard the rumours about Hollow Creek Church. The old structure, abandoned since the 1800s, was said to be cursed—its final sermon interrupted by a priest who burned alive at the altar, screaming scripture as the flames consumed him.

Armed with torches and bravado, they broke in through a shattered stained-glass window one stormy night. In the centre of the chancel, beneath layers of old dust, they found a rusted trapdoor. "Dare you," Jordan grinned.

Beneath the church lay a crypt—not on any map they had looked at, possibly undocumented, hidden even from history. At the far end, carved into the stone, was a strange altar with ancient markings neither of them recognised. A stone tablet with ancient text carved into it rested in the centre.

Eli ran his hand over it. The words looked twisted and difficult to read, yet they felt like something more sinister—almost a warning, or perhaps, an invitation. Against their better judgment, they read a passage aloud. The wind died. The storm outside stopped mid-thunderclap. And from the centre of the altar, a hand reached out—black, clawed, and burning with a fire that didn't give off light, only darkness. The devil hadn't been banished to Hell; he had been sealed. And they had just set him free. The being that emerged was powerful beyond all belief.

Within days, the world began to rot. Hospitals overflowed with patients whose skin blistered with heatless burns. Crops turned to cinders overnight. Animals grew feral and chaotic, screaming as if tormented by unseen flames. The air itself began to shimmer with a fever. The Burning Plague, they called it.

But there was no cure. No containment. The devil walked the earth in human form—eyes like molten rock, a smile carved from torment—spreading fire with a touch, sinking venomous promises into the ears of leaders and children alike.

And Eli and Jordan? They were spared—but not saved. Marked by the curse, they became his Heralds, burning with a slow internal flame, doomed to walk behind him, spreading ash in his name. The last thing Eli remembered before losing himself to the fire was a line from the priest's journal they found later, buried beneath the church: "The devil cannot be killed. But he can be bound.

By blood. By fire. And by the innocence of those who set him free." It ended with one chilling warning, scribbled in panic: "If you are reading this, it is already too late."

The world was ash now. Cities fell in silence, not to war or screams, but to a heatless fire that turned steel to smoke and bone to black glass. The devil walked in daylight without fear, dressed in human skin stitched from those who dared resist. He had a name once, but now he was only called The Ember King.

Eli and Jordan followed, shadows behind the flame, their bodies intact but their minds fractured. They were more than human now—flesh bound to ember, cursed to live with burning lungs and sleepless nights. Wherever they walked, fire spread. Grass curled and died. Children cried in silence, staring at them like ghosts.

But somewhere, deep inside, the last flicker of who they were refused to go out. It started with a dream. Eli saw the priest again—the one who had burned alive on the altar a century ago. But this time, the priest wasn't screaming. He was calling out: "There is still a way."

"Blood. Fire. Innocence."

Eli woke, coughing black smoke, his hands glowing faintly with a fire that didn't burn his skin.

He found Jordan staring at the sky, where clouds bled like wounded animals. "I think we were chosen," Jordan muttered. "Not by him. By something older."

The dream came again. And again. Until they understood. The priest hadn't died in vain. He had sacrificed himself—blood, fire, and innocence—to trap the devil beneath Hollow Creek. His soul, bound within the Codex Daemonium, whispered to those who would listen. Eli and Jordan had released the devil. Now they had to bind him again. The cost would be the same.

The Ember King knew. As they neared the place where it had all begun, the world burned brighter behind them. Their own skin cracked with glowing red lines. The devil watched them from afar, amused—not angry. He thought he knew how this ended.

Back beneath the church, in the black crypt, the altar still stood. The Codex lay open, waiting. Eli took a blade. Jordan went to the inscribed stone. They read the passage again—but backwards. They let their blood fall onto the altar, its embers hissing. And Jordan, tears running down his ash-streaked face, spoke aloud: "I'm sorry." He threw himself onto the altar.

Innocence. Fire. Blood. The world screamed. The Ember King roared in fury as his body shattered into burning cinders. The flames recoiled from the earth like breath sucked back into lungs.

And then… silence fell.

When Eli woke, the world was dim, the sky overcast—not with ash, but with real clouds. Rain began to fall for the first time in months. It was cool and pure, carrying a feeling of hope. He was alone. But in the distance, where fire once ruled, green had begun to grow. The Codex Daemonium was gone.

But legends don't die. Some say the Ember King still waits, trapped once more—but weakened. And others say Eli walks the world now, carrying the last embers of the curse inside him, guarding the balance between fire and salvation. Because the devil wasn't destroyed, merely sleeping. And one day, someone else might read the wrong words again.

Part 2

The Spark

It's been fifty years since the sky cleared. The world remembers the Burning Plague like a nightmare— half-real, half-legend. The official records call it "The Global Firestorm Anomaly," an unexplained phenomenon. But survivors, the few who were old enough to truly see, still whisper one name in fear: The Ember King.

Most people don't believe in him anymore. But Emberwatch does. Formed in secret, scattered across continents, Emberwatch is a shadow network of scholars, hunters, and descendants of those who bore the mark of the fire. At its centre is a girl named Nova.

Sixteen years old. A foster kid. Sharp as a blade. She has a scar on her left shoulder shaped like a flame. She doesn't know who her parents were. She doesn't know why strange fires seem to erupt in her wake. But she dreams of a man with burning eyes and a voice that calls her "the spark."

One day, while exploring an off-limits sector of the ruins beneath Old Hollow Creek—now a fenced-off nature preserve—Nova finds something impossible: a page. Brittle. Bound in black leather.

From the Codex Daemonium. The writing seems to move when she looks at it. The moment her fingers brush the ink, she hears it: a call from the stone beneath her feet. "Blood. Fire. Innocence. Again."

Later that night, an entire city block burns down without a single match being struck. She wakes up miles away, unharmed, the mark on her shoulder glowing red.

The Ember King is not sleeping. He's waiting. Waiting for the right vessel. One born from flame. One tied to the bloodline of those who first freed him—and bound him again. Nova. She doesn't know yet, but Eli was her grandfather. The fire runs in her veins. And now the Codex wants her.

Emberwatch tries to stop it, tries to hide her. But fire can't be hidden. Soon, others awaken—The Cinderborn—marked by the flame, drawn to Nova, twisted by the old power reawakening beneath the earth. The seals are breaking. And Nova will have to decide: will she finish what her family started? Or become the vessel that brings the Ember King back—for good?

The world burns again. Not slowly this time— suddenly. Cities are swallowed in seconds. Oceans boil. The moon turns red. And at the centre of it all stands Nova, eyes like wildfire, arms outstretched as the earth splits beneath her.

She fought it, tried for months to deny her nature. But you can't run from blood. You can't outrun a curse woven into your bones before you were born.

All the while, the seal was weakening. The Ember King, reaching from the shadow between life and death, seduced her not with fear—but with understanding. "You are not the end," he whispered. "You are the beginning." And when the last page of the Codex caught flame in her hands, she didn't scream. She smiled. For the first time, she felt whole.

The Ember King didn't need to possess her. She became him. The vessel, the bloodline, the innocence twisted into power—everything now aligned. The fire didn't just return. It evolved. Emberwatch fell one by one, burning to nothing. The Cinderborn rose with her, flame-eyed disciples who had waited generations for a true heir. Beneath Hollow Creek, the stone altar cracked wide open—revealing not a crypt, but a gate.

One last time, the world hoped. They sent one man—Eli, older than human years should allow, still alive, barely. His soul scorched, held together by regret and ritual. He carried a knife made from Jordan's bones. He stepped into the firestorm to reach her. And she remembered him.

"Grandfather."

His voice was broken when he spoke. "You can still stop this."

Nova looked at him with eyes that weren't hers anymore. "I don't want to stop it."

"But this isn't you—"

"No," she said, her voice a chorus of smoke and flame. "This is exactly me." She kissed his forehead, and he burst into ash.

With that, the last resistance crumbled. The seal shattered. The underworld rose to meet the surface, not in chaos—but in order. Cities built of black stone and burning glass. A throne of molten bone atop the ruins of what was once Hollow Creek. The Ember King didn't return to the world. He was the world now.

And Nova, once a girl, now a god of flames, sat on that throne and watched the sky turn black with smoke. The final line of the Codex Daemonium, once hidden, now burned across the stars: "When innocence is lost and the bloodline consumed, the fire shall no longer burn the world. It shall become it."

Chapter 25

Web of Silence

Nobody really noticed when Mia stopped speaking. It started subtly. One day she just… didn't answer a question in class. Her lips parted slightly, but no words came out. Her eyes darted, terrified. The teacher thought it was just nerves. But Mia knew better. She'd felt them moving again. Crawling just beneath her tongue.

The curse began on her sixteenth birthday. A gift from a stranger in a tattered coat who approached her at the cemetery where her mother was buried. He said something to her in a language she didn't understand and pressed a tiny glass jar into her hand. Inside was a single, black spider, its legs twitching.

That night, Mia woke up choking. She stumbled to the mirror and opened her mouth—and the spider scuttled out from under her tongue, trailing a fine, silvery silk. She screamed, but only webs came out.

Every day since, more began to emerge from her throat. From the pit of her stomach. Tiny, gleaming eyes, twitching legs, dripping mandibles. They would crawl out of her mouth when she was alone, skittering across the floor and vanishing into the walls. Mia learned to keep quiet. Learned to swallow hard when she felt them climbing up her oesophagus. But they were growing.

At school, the spiders began to show themselves—scurrying across desks, descending from ceilings, spinning thick webs in lockers. Students laughed at first. Then they screamed. Then they started to disappear. A caretaker was the first. Found wrapped in silk behind the boiler room, mummified and drained. Then a group of students vanished after teasing Mia during lunch. All that remained were their phones—each one showing a video of Mia with her mouth slowly opening, and hundreds of hairy black legs spilling out.

Now the school is sealed off. Police tape, news vans, police in forensic suits. But nobody knows where Mia is. Some say she's hiding in the ventilation system. Some say she's dead. But the survivors—what few are left—swear they still hear her, somewhere in the darkened corridors, spinning her webs.

The school became abandoned through the investigation, wrapped in silence like a corpse in silk. A rot had set in, thick and sweet, as if the building itself were decaying from the inside out. The police never spoke about what they found on the third floor. About the officer who went in with a search dog and never came back. Or the dog, found days later, hollowed out like a puppet, still twitching with something moving inside. They closed the case, tried to keep it quiet and not scare the public. Called it gas leaks, mould, structural instability. It was all lies, we knew it. Everyone in town knew the truth, even if they never said it aloud.

Mia's father went in last. Desperate and armed with a torch, a crowbar, and a letter Mia had written the night before she disappeared. "They're part of me now," she'd scrawled in frantic, jagged handwriting. "I can't hold them in much longer. They don't sleep. And they're hungry."

He found the door to the library fused shut with webbing so thick it looked like muscle tissue. He hacked through it, coughing as dust and spores filled his lungs. The silence inside was suffocating—too perfect. Then he heard it, a wet clicking, like chitin on tile. He shone the torch on the lockers. Every single one… was pulsing. A sound like breathing. Inside, something scraped.

The torch flickered and went out. And in the dark, he heard her voice.
"Mia?" he shouted. "No," it said.

The light snapped back on. She was standing at the end of the hallway. Pale. Hair hanging like drowned moss. Her eyes were gone—replaced by clusters of gleaming black orbs. Her mouth twitched. Then opened.

Spiders poured out like a black, rushing flood. Not dozens. Not hundreds. Thousands. Some no bigger than a thumbnail. Others the size of dinner plates. Their bodies glistened with wet silk and the scent of decay. They swarmed over him before he could scream, their legs scratching in secrets against his skin as they burrowed into his mouth, his ears, his eyes. He was still screaming when they stitched his lips shut with web.

Now, every few nights, shapes move behind the windows in the school. A child swears she saw a girl watching her from the third floor too. Just smiling and starring. Sometimes, the wind carries a sound like hissing. Sometimes it's laughter. And if you get close enough to the old gym doors… you might hear the faint rustle of a thousand legs. Waiting for you to become it's pray.

The story didn't stop their though, there was more to it as time went on, the web of suffering spun further and further. It was supposed to be a joke. A stupid Halloween dare. Lena Cruz didn't even want to go into the old school. But when you're the new girl, trying to survive your first year without being invisible, sometimes you do stupid things.

Things like following a bunch of immature teenagers into a building that's been sealed off for two years.

"Chickening out already?" Jayden laughed, "Thought you were from the city."
Lena rolled her eyes. "The city has rats and serial killers. Not… ghost schools."

They climbed through a broken window. Inside, the air was warm and wet. The kind of damp that made your clothes cling and your skin itch. Every surface was coated in a fine dust that wasn't dust—it was web. Pale. Dry. Like it had been growing there for decades.

They moved through the corridors, their phone torches slicing thin beams through the gloom. Every time Lena's light swept across a locker, she could swear it moved. Just a little. "Let's find the prayer room," Jayden said, grinning. "That's where they found the body."

"Which one?" someone whispered behind them. No one answered. The group thinned out as they went deeper. Only Lena, Jayden, and a girl named Bri stuck to the plan. They made it to the third floor, the door to the library still warped with layers of web that looked more like scar tissue than silk. "Hell no," Bri said, backing away. "This place is weird, something is definitely wrong here."

But Jayden was already cutting through the web with a hunting knife. "Don't be a baby." He broke through and the door creaked open. Blackness spilled out like a fog.

The prayer room was a void of web. Every shelf dripped with it, sagging under the weight. Bones poked through strands like broken marionettes. Lena stepped forward, torch trembling. "Jayden…" she whispered. "Do you hear that?"

A soft shuddering. Like dry leaves scraping across tile. Then something else—almost like a giggle. Jayden turned, ready to crack another joke. But it wasn't Lena laughing. Something behind him was.

Bri screamed. Jayden spun around—and the torchlight caught her just for a moment. A girl standing between the shelves. Her head tilted too far to the side. Her mouth—oh god, her mouth—hung open, unhinged. And from it came a cascade of legs, eyes, and fangs.

Jayden dropped his torch. It hit the floor and went out. Then came the feeding.

Lena didn't scream. She couldn't. She ran— slipping, sliding through webs and slime, down stairwells where shadows twitched just out of reach. She burst through the window they'd come in through and tumbled into the grass, sobbing and covered in silk. She was the only one who made it out.

Now she dreams of Mia. Every night. The spiders crawl across her skin. Into her ears. Down her throat. She wakes up choking, with tiny, star-shaped bites along her lips and fine webs on her pillow. And the worst part? Sometimes, she hears them speak: "You're one of us now."

Mia didn't remember what it was like to be human. Not really. She remembered flashes—her mother's perfume, the feeling of grass between her fingers, a birthday cake. But those memories were dusty now, half-eaten by the hunger that lived inside her. The spiders had taken root. At first, she was their host. Now, she was their queen.

She slept beneath the school, in the boiler room—though it wasn't a room anymore. It was a nest. Webs clung to every pipe, pulsing gently with warmth and life. Egg sacs lined the walls, twitching with motion. Some were small. Others… bigger than dogs. They were changing. Evolving. Feeding on what she gave them.

Every time a new trespasser entered the school, Mia knew. She felt them like vibrations in a web— every footstep, every breath. She could taste their fear in the air. It fed her children. Kept the hive strong. She walked barefoot now, her skin pale and silken, veins like dark threads beneath the surface.

Her eyes had become something else entirely—faceted, shimmering in the dark. She didn't blink. She didn't need to. When she opened her mouth now, it was no longer just a scream—it was a summoning.

But lately, something was wrong. A tug in the web. A signal she hadn't made. She thought it was the girl who'd escaped. Lena. The one whose blood was laced with silk, whose dreams dripped with hatchlings. She'd been marked, after all. Mia had let her go on purpose. A seed to plant in the outside world. But this wasn't Lena. This was something older. Something moving beneath her nest.

Late one night, Mia descended through a hidden door behind the old canteen, deeper than she'd ever gone before. The air grew colder. The silk grew thicker. Stranger. It wasn't hers. She found it at the bottom of a tunnel so dark her spiders wouldn't follow. A wall of web, black as pitch, knotted with symbols—runes that moved when she looked at them. And in the centre, a hole. Something inside it, breathing. It spoke without sound. A language older than her curse. Older than death.

"You are the vessel. But you are not the end."

Mia staggered back. For the first time in years, she felt something foreign inside her: fear. From the hole, a leg began to emerge. Too long. Too many joints. Not hers. Something was coming. Something ancient. And she was just the beginning.

It unfurled from the darkness like smoke through a graveyard. The thing in the tunnel—The Weaver Beneath—had no name spoken by human tongues. It moved in silence, older than rot, older than light, older than death itself. Where Mia's brood scuttled and twitched, this one glided, its legs sliding across stone as if the world itself made way for it.

It had slept for centuries beneath what used to be forest, then church, then school. Buried beneath stone and ignorance. Forgotten by time. Until Mia woke it. Until her body, her curse, her spiders had spun the perfect invitation. It had heard her song.

Mia stumbled backwards from the hole, breath catching in her throat. Her children hissed and curled away, instinctively knowing this creature was not kin. Not predator. Not prey. It was the spider god!

Chapter 26

Meat Market

There's a local butcher's shop just two streets down from Ravensfield college. You've probably passed it—"Holloway & Sons," with its old, creaky sign and windows fogged over with condensation, even when it's not cold. Most kids at school just call it "The Meat Locker."

It's run by two brothers, Walter and Dean Holloway—big, pale men with thick hands, almost always seen in bloodstained aprons. They inherited the place from their father, who disappeared decades ago under mysterious circumstances. Some say he went mad, others say he was taken... but no one really talks about it anymore.

What they do talk about—quietly, when teachers aren't around—is how students from Ravensfield have been going missing over the years. First, it was Jared Collins. Vanished walking home after detention. Then Rachel Li. She'd mentioned she was stopping by Holloway's to get bones for her dog. Then Lucas White, who had a part-time job sweeping up at the shop. The police found nothing. The Holloways were "cooperative." No signs of foul play.

But the weirdest part? Ever since those disappearances started… the school lunches got better. Way better. The burgers were juicier. The stew was rich and thick, no longer the watery mess they used to serve. People started queuing up for seconds. It was all "locally sourced meat," the dinner lady said, "generously donated by the community." No one questioned it. No one wanted to.

Except for Katie Marlow. She was on the school paper, a real investigative type. Started asking around. Snuck into the kitchen after hours. Said she saw crates marked "Holloway & Sons" stacked in the freezer—no labels, just vacuum-sealed packets of meat. One of them was labelled with a name: "J. Collins." She told her friends she was going to confront the butchers. That was Friday. She never came back to school, she is still classed as a missing person.

Monday, the lunch special was "Pulled Pork Sandwiches." Everyone said they were the best yet.

Now there's a new sign at the butcher's: "Hiring – After-School Help Wanted. Good Pay."

Think twice before you apply, the joke around the school was. There is more to this story too, more strange accounts that something suspicious is going on, and Holloway & Sons are hiding a dark secret.

Part 2

The One Who Got Away

My name is Eli Granger, and I should be dead. I was in the same year as Katie Marlow. She sat behind me in English, always scribbling in the margins of her books—half poetry, half crime scene analysis. She was obsessed with the disappearances. When she vanished, I knew the Holloways were behind it.

The police didn't believe me. My parents told me to shut up and stop spreading conspiracy theories. But I couldn't let it go. I had to know what happened to her. So I did something no one else had dared—I got hired. Told Walter I wanted after-school work. He just looked me up and down and smiled, a slow and heavy expression. "We've got a place for you," he said.

They had me carry boxes, clean saws, mop the floor. I kept my head down and waited. Until one night, I followed Dean through a back door I wasn't supposed to notice, down into a sub-basement behind the walk-in freezer.

It wasn't a storage room. It was… a butcher's chapel. Hooks hung from the ceiling, some still swaying gently. The walls were covered in tally marks, scratched in with fingernails. In the corner—coolers. Labelled by name. One of them was hers. Katie.

That's when Dean saw me. He came at me with the bone saw. I ran—slipped in something wet, screamed, scrambled—and barely made it up the stairs. I locked him down there. I set the place on fire. Every drop of kerosene I could find. But they survived and damage was minimal. The fire department found no trace of bodies. Just "animal bones."

Holloway & Sons reopened within 2 weeks like nothing ever happened. No one believes my story, but it's true. I carry the scars—both on my shoulder and in my nightmares. If you're reading this, stay away from that butcher's shop. They're still hungry.

Part 3

The Hunt Begins

Detective Clara Fields had been with Ravensfield Police service for nineteen years. She'd seen it all—drug overdoses, domestic abuse, even a cult once, operating out of a shuttered nail bar. But the Holloway case? That was different.

The files were messy. Incomplete. Witness reports

vanished. Evidence was destroyed in "freak accidents." The missing kids? Officially labelled "runaways," every last one of them. But Fields remembered them. Jared. Rachel. Lucas. Katie. And now, a new name: Eli Granger. The only survivor. Scarred, paranoid, living off-grid with family. She tracked him down in a caravan six towns over.

He showed her the journal Katie had left behind—pages full of names, meat cuts, shipping routes, and one sentence written over and over again: WE ARE WHAT WE EAT.

Fields reopened the case unofficially. She started digging into health department records, cafeteria suppliers, the Holloway family tree. That's when she discovered the most chilling part: The Holloways had no birth certificates. No marriage licences. No property deeds. Nothing. According to the state, they didn't exist. And yet, their meat kept showing up. Not just at Ravensfield High, but at six different schools across the region.

She followed a delivery truck one night. It didn't go to a slaughterhouse. It drove deep into the woods, to a cold storage facility with no signage. She's been missing ever since. The last thing found at her desk was a file marked "ACTIVE INVESTIGATION." Inside was a map, a butcher's cleaver wrapped in cloth, and a note that simply read: "They've been feeding us for over a century. And we've thanked them for it."

Part 4

The Final Harvest

The Holloway brothers have been around for over a century. They are not just butchers. They are hunters. And Ravensfield has been their hunting ground for generations.

Clara Fields had barely begun to piece together the terrifying puzzle when she vanished. Her file was the last thread, and when it was buried, the case went cold. But Eli Granger, the survivor, started to remember things he'd buried in avoidance and isolation. The truth clawed its way back when he found Clara's final notes. The last piece fell into place.

It all started in 1911. Ravensfield's dark past was built on the blood of its early settlers, the Holloway family among them. The brothers Walter and Dean were not just men. They were descendants of a long-forgotten cult that had made a pact with something ancient—something that needed flesh to survive. They didn't just inherit the butcher's shop;

they took it, along with the town, and made it their centre of operations.

The disappearances weren't random. They were a slow, methodical harvest, dating back to the first decade of the 20th century. Each missing person was a ritual. A payment. A sacrifice. The Holloways kept it quiet because no one dared question them.

Eli gathered a group of older survivors he contacted online—those few who had escaped the Holloway web previously. They were the ones who remembered the faces of the missing. The ones who still felt the weight of what they had eaten. They snuck back into the town, where Holloway & Sons was still open, the smell of smoked meat hanging in the air. This time, it didn't smell appetising. It smelled like death.

The survivors brought fire. They descended into the basement, armed with the knowledge Fields had uncovered. Inside the cellar, they found it all: the stacks of butchered bodies, the rows of frozen packages, the labels marked with names and dates like an inventory. At the far end, behind a hidden door, lay something more horrific than they could have imagined.

Walter and Dean weren't just keeping the town fed. They were keeping something alive. In the back room was a portal—an ancient, pulsating altar of bone and flesh. Around it, statues of monstrous, forgotten gods watched as the Holloways chanted in a language older than time. The altar was their true business.

"You can't kill us," Walter said, his voice like gravel, heavy with centuries of sin. "We are the harvest. You are the harvest."

The altar flared to life. The walls began to bleed, the floor cracked open, and horrors crawled out from the depths. Eli grabbed the cleaver from the table—the one Fields had left behind—and swung it at the altar, shattering the pulsating stone.

The room screamed. The Holloways lunged, but they were too late. The portal collapsed, and in that moment, Ravensfield was freed. The butcher's shop and the unspeakable horrors within were swallowed by the earth itself.

Eli left the town, moving as far away as he could, where the smell of smoked meat couldn't reach him. Growing older he built a new life, found a job, and even started to dream of normalcy again. But every night, the dreams returned. The smell of blood. The ringing bell. The cold, damp air of the butcher's basement. He'd wake up in a cold sweat, the echoes of Walter's voice in his head: "We are the harvest. And you will feed us again."

It was just a nightmare, he told himself. But one

night, while walking home, he noticed something strange. A new butcher's shop had just opened in the centre of town. A clean, modern sign hung above the door: "Holloway's Butcher & Deli."

He froze. His heart pounded. No. It can't be. They're gone!

But the door opened, and a man stepped out. Tall, broad-shouldered, with an unmistakable smile. It was Walter Holloway. Eerily untouched by time. And in his hands? A butcher's cleaver.

"Eli," Walter said, his voice low and thick with that same unsettling calm. "You never really leave. Not forever. You'll be hungry again. And when you are…" He stepped aside, revealing the sign that glinted under the evening sun. Beneath the pristine words "Holloway's Butcher & Deli" was a smaller, faded label, as if scrawled in dried blood: Freshly Sourced. Locally Fed.

Eli's stomach twisted. And in the reflection of the butcher's window, he saw something that made his blood run cold. Standing just behind Walter, eyes glowing like embers, was Dean Holloway. In the reflection of the glass, Eli saw the truth. The Holloways had never died. The ritual had only moved.

And he, like so many before him, would become part of the next harvest.

Chapter 27

The Whispering Pines Captives

The scent of pine and damp earth filled Maya's lungs, a welcome change from the city's ceaseless vibe. Beside her, Liam wrestled with a stubborn tent pole, his grunts echoing faintly in the serene evening air. Chloe, ever the organiser, meticulously arranged their campfire supplies, humming a tuneless melody. Behind them, Noah, their resident cynic, remained glued to his phone screen, muttering darkly about the abysmal signal.

It was their annual "escape the parents" camping trip, a cherished ritual, this year deep in the supposedly tranquil heart of the Whispering Pines National Forest – a place rumoured to hold ancient secrets that usually only surfaced in ghost stories.

The first two days were idyllic. They hiked winding trails where sunlight dappled through the dense canopy, told increasingly terrible jokes around a crackling fire, and roasted marshmallows until they were blackened, sugary husks. The forest felt alive, a comforting presence.

But on the third night, as twilight deepened into an inky blackness, a strange and unnerving mist began to roll in. It was incredibly thick, obscuring vision within mere feet and carrying an almost metallic chill that seemed to seep into their very bones. It swirled around their campsite, tendrils snaking eerily between their tents, extinguishing the warmth of their fire faster than the night air should.

And with the mist came the chants. The sounds were ancient and raw, coiling through the air from everywhere and nowhere at once, a low, they grew steadily louder, more defined, and more unsettling.

"Anyone else hear that?" Chloe spoke out, her eyes alert with a fear that mirrored Maya's own.

Liam gripped a fallen branch, his usual bravado gone. "Sounds… old," he murmured, his gaze darting frantically into the swirling grey. "Really old. Like, tribal old."

Before they could comprehend the chilling implication, figures began to materialise from the shifting mist. They weren't solid, but shimmering, translucent forms, their edges indistinct as if constantly dissolving and reforming. They were armed with archaic spears and bows that seemed woven from shadow and moonlight, yet cast no shadows of their own. Their eyes, or where eyes should have been, burned with an eerie, phosphorescent light, fixating on the stunned teens with an ancient, predatory intelligence.

Their movements were impossibly swift,

unnervingly silent, a fluid, gliding motion that defied physics. They were numerous, an overwhelming presence emerging from the very depths of the forest itself.

A scream caught in Maya's throat. Her muscles locked, then jolted into raw, desperate instinct. They scattered, each teen bolting in a different direction. But the ghostly warriors were too fast, too ethereal. Maya felt a sudden, cold, intangible grip on her arm, a touch that sent shivers of ice through her veins despite its lack of physical presence, pulling her with relentless strength into the thickening mist. The last thing she saw before the grey swallowed her completely was Noah's terrified face as he too was dragged away by another shimmering, silent figure.

They were thrown into a makeshift enclosure, not a cage of bars, but a clearing surrounded by ancient, moss-covered stones that shimmered with the same ethereal energy as their captors. The air within was heavy and oppressive, filled with the scent of damp decay and something else— something electric and cold, like the static before a lightning strike.

As their eyes adjusted, they saw other captives: spectral, silent figures resembling people from vastly different eras—a pioneer in buckskin, a Victorian woman in a tattered gown, a child in archaic clothing. Their faces were etched with a timeless despair, their ghostly eyes reflecting nothing. It was then the teens realised the horrifying truth: these were not living people who had been captured recently. They were ghosts too, just like their captors, held in the same spectral prison, perhaps for centuries.

Days bled into indistinguishable stretches of mist-shrouded limbo. Time seemed to warp, stretching thin then snapping back, marked only by the shifting intensity of the mist outside and the slow erosion of their hope. The ghostly tribe would occasionally observe them, their glowing eyes unreadable, their silence more terrifying than any overt threat. Their torment was a constant, unsettling tone that continued relentlessly, pushing them to the edges of their sanity. They huddled together, their conversations reduced to minimum, their fear a constant, suffocating companion. Hunger and thirst became distant sensations, less pressing than the gnawing despair of their ethereal confinement.

Then, one "night" – though night and day were indistinguishable – a profound and absolute silence descended. The oppressive chants stopped abruptly. The heavy, cold feeling in the air lifted completely, replaced by an unsettling emptiness. Cautiously, Liam peered through the translucent barriers of their prison.

The ghostly tribe was gone. Not vanished, not dissolved, but simply gone. The clearing was utterly empty. It was as if they had never existed.

The mist itself began to thin rapidly, swirling away to reveal the familiar, solid trees of Pines, now bathed in the silvery light of the late moon. They stumbled out, disoriented and shaken to their core. Trembling, they found their campsite, abandoned but miraculously untouched, their tents and backpacks mockingly mundane, as if nothing out of the ordinary had occurred.

They never spoke of it in detail again, not really, not even among themselves. How could they? Who would believe they had been captured by ghosts who were themselves ancient echoes, and then, those spirits had simply... disappeared. Vanished without a trace, leaving behind only the chilling memory of their glowing eyes and the phantom echoes of ancient chants that would forever resonate in the deepest corners of their minds. The Whispering Pines, once a place of escape, now held a terrifying, unspoken secret: a stark reminder of a tribe that was there, then wasn't, a chilling mystery forever embedded in the silent, ancient woods.

Chapter 28

The Unexplained Abduction

The annoying low hum from the assembly hall always made Noah's teeth ache, a dull, persistent vibration that resonated deep within his jaw. Another mundane Tuesday, another droning lecture on "future readiness" from Principal Albright, whose impossibly wide, unwavering smile seemed surgically affixed to her face, a mask of perpetual, unsettling cheer. Beside him, Chloe, usually a whirlwind of restless energy, found solace in the methodical scratching of her pen, her intricate doodles blooming across her notebook page, a silent rebellion against the monotony.

Liam, ever the restless spirit, tapped a silent, frantic rhythm on his knee, his eyes darting around the cavernous hall as if searching for an escape route, a glimpse of anything less predictable. It was a perfectly ordinary morning at Northwood school, a sprawling fortress of drab brick and institutional blandness, a place where nothing truly extraordinary, nothing truly alarming, ever happened. Until it did.

The first sign was subtle, almost too insignificant to register: a barely perceptible blink in the overhead lights, a momentary stutter in their harsh, steady glow. Then, a low, resonant thrum began, not quite a sound, but a vibration that seemed to emanate from beneath the very foundation of the hall, vibrating through the floor, up through their chairs, and settling deep in their chests cavities, a disquieting internal tremor. Principal Albright's voice, mid-sentence, faltered, her fixed smile briefly twitching, a microscopic crack in her perfect facade. A faint, almost sickly green light, luminous and unnaturally vibrant, began to bleed through the sealed, reinforced windows, casting a strange glow on the sea of stunned, confused faces in the hall. It painted the beige walls in an unsettling, otherworldly hue. A collective gasp, barely stifled, rippled through the student body, a wave of unease and growing fear.

Suddenly, the hum intensified, rising in pitch and volume, peaking into a deafening, piercing shriek that clawed at their eardrums, a sound so agonisingly high-pitched it felt as though their very skulls might crack. A blinding flash of pure, emerald light, what felt like something brighter than a thousand suns, filled the room, so potent it seemed to burn behind their eyelids even when squeezed shut–leaving ghostly green afterimages dancing in their vision. When it subsided, the silence that followed was absolute, crushing, heavier than the oppressive hum had been, a vacuum of sound that pressed in on them. And in that profound, ringing silence, as their eyes struggled to adjust, they noticed.

Jessica Chen, the school's seemingly invincible star athlete, wasn't in her seat in the front row. Her perfectly organised backpack still slumped beside the chair, but Jessica herself was simply gone. Neither was Alex Miller, the quiet, almost invisible kid from their english class, whose textbooks lay open on his desk. Two empty spaces, two perfectly aligned rows of bewildered students staring at nothing but the suddenly vacant chairs. The principal, after a moment of stunned, unsettling silence where her gaze seemed to drift unfocused, cleared her throat with an almost mechanical precision, her voice regaining its artificial, sickeningly sweet cheer. "Just a minor power surge, folks! Nothing to worry about! Let's get back to... our discussion on biology!" She clapped her hands together, the sound unnaturally loud in the silent hall.

But it wasn't a power surge. Noah knew it, a cold certainty settling in his gut. Chloe knew it, her wide eyes locked onto the empty seats. Liam knew it, his nervous tapping having ceased entirely. The talking started immediately, soft at first, then spreading like a virus through the hall, morphing into frantic, hushed questions: Jessica? Alex? Where did they go? Did they just… disappear? The fear was palpable, a live thing buzzing in the air, but somehow, the teachers seemed immune.

The school's response was swift, coordinated, and unsettlingly unified. Within minutes, an announcement blared over the intercom: Jessica and Alex had been "called home due to urgent family emergencies." Their lockers were emptied with suspicious, almost unnatural speed by janitors who usually moved at a glacial pace. Their names vanished from attendance sheets, from the sports roster, from the debate club sign-up, as if they had never existed.

Most chillingly, the teachers, usually a chaotic, endearing blend of eccentric personalities, became unnervingly uniform, their individual quirks flattened into a disturbingly placid homogeneity. Mr Harrison, their perpetually grumpy history teacher, whose lectures were usually punctuated by cynical sighs, now greeted students with an unsettlingly placid, almost glassy smile.

Ms Davies, the scatterbrained art teacher who frequently had paint on her face, now spoke with a newfound, rigid clarity, her voice devoid of its usual melodic chaos. Their eyes, once so varied in expression—some twinkling with mischief, others narrowed in concentration, still others dulled by exhaustion—now held a detached, almost reflective quality, like still ponds mirroring the sky. They were too calm, too watchful, their gazes lingering a moment too long on any student who dared to question the disappearances, a silent, unnerving warning.

"Something's seriously wrong," Chloe whispered to Noah during lunch, pushing her untouched tray of mystery meat and limp vegetables away, the usual cafeteria vibe seeming muted and distant. "They're acting like... like robots, or puppets. All their little quirks are just gone." The vibrant life that usually animated their teachers had been replaced by a chilling stillness.

Liam, who had initially scoffed at Noah's nascent "alien abduction" theories, his cynicism slowly eroding, nodded slowly, his own sandwich forgotten. "Did you see Mr Evans in chemistry? He just stared at the Bunsen burner for like, five minutes straight. Didn't even blink. Just... stared." His voice was barely a murmur, laced with a fear he rarely showed.

Noah, always analytical, felt a cold knot tighten in his stomach, a logical terror that resonated with his observations. The teachers weren't just acting weird; they were acting too normal, a perfected veneer that screamed artifice, a meticulous imitation of human behaviour. "It's the uniformity that's really creeping me out," he murmured, picking at a loose thread on his jeans. "And how quickly they shut down any talk about Jessica or Alex. It's like they've been programmed."

Their investigation began subtly, almost accidentally, driven by a growing sense of wrongness. Chloe, with her sharp artistic eye, was the first to stumble upon a tangible clue. During an after-school art club, she noticed a strange, repeating symbol etched almost imperceptibly into the corner of Principal Albright's massive, oak desk, barely visible under a stack of official-looking papers.

It was a complex, interlocking geometric pattern, angular yet fluid, unlike anything she'd ever seen in any art history book or cultural text. It seemed alien, both ancient and futuristic at once. Liam, surprisingly adept at picking locks (a skill reluctantly acquired during a brief, misguided phase of aspiring to be a master illusionist), managed to get them into the faculty lounge after hours. It was sterile, unnervingly tidy, stripped of the usual coffee stains and crumpled papers, but what caught his eye were the pristine white hazmat suits hanging neatly in an unused closet, complete with strange, tinted visors that seemed to obscure more than protect. Why, in a normal secondary school, would teachers need what looked like advanced biohazard gear?

Noah, meanwhile, spent hours in the internet, ostensibly studying for upcoming exams, but covertly observing the movements and behaviours of the school. He noticed a peculiar pattern in teacher absences and reappearances, always occurring within hours after one of the green glow incidents that no one else seemed to recall, incidents that he now remembered with chilling clarity. He also found a forgotten, ancient-looking textbook on obscure, unpronounceable languages on Mr Harrison's desk, tucked beneath a stack of bland curriculum guides. The book was filled with marginalia—notes scribbled in that same strange, interlocking symbols Chloe had found on the principal's desk. The script was spiky, elegant, and profoundly wrong.

The disparate pieces slowly began to click into a terrifying mosaic, forming a picture far more sinister than any of them had imagined. One afternoon, while retrieving a forgotten textbook from his locker, Noah overheard a hushed, clipped conversation drifting from the slightly ajar staff room door. "...the next phase of acclimatisation is crucial. Their integration must be seamless before the harvest." It was Mr Evans' voice, usually booming with forced cheer, but now colder, devoid of his usual jocularity, flat and devoid of warmth. "And the parameters for the next subject... more resistant this time. The children are adapting too quickly to the inhibitors. We need to refine the sedatives."

The children are adapting too quickly. The words echoed in Noah's mind, a chilling confirmation of his darkest fears, chilling him to the bone. Inhibitors. Sedatives. The disappearances weren't random acts of running away or transfers. The students weren't runaways. And the teachers… the teachers weren't just covering it up. They were part of it. They were complicit. The thought of Mr Harrison, who'd taught them about freedom and rebellion, his voice passionate, or Ms Davies, who'd encouraged their wild creativity with such enthusiasm, being involved in such a sinister plot, sent a wave of acidic nausea through him. His world, once predictable and safe, was twisting into a grotesque nightmare.

He quickly relayed every chilling detail of what he'd heard to Chloe and Liam, their faces paling dramatically in the dim, dust-moted light of the empty classroom they'd chosen as their clandestine meeting spot, their sanctuary. The implications were horrifying, unfathomable. Their trusted educators, the adults responsible for their safety, the figures of authority they had always implicitly relied upon, were either controlled by, or actively collaborating with, whatever monstrous entities were behind the abductions. And the word "harvest"… it hung in the air between them, thick and suffocating, like a death knell tolling for their entire generation. What did these creatures harvest? Their minds? Their bodies? Their very souls? The possibilities were too terrible to contemplate.

Their next move was incredibly risky, born of desperation. They decided to directly target Ms Davies. She was small, seemed the most physically vulnerable, and her recent, jarring change in demeanour—from flighty artist to rigid automaton—was the most unsettlingly obvious. They decided to follow her after school, hoping she would lead them to more answers, or perhaps, a way out. They trailed her old, dented sedan through the quiet suburban streets, its familiar shape now radiating an aura of dread. They watched as she drove not to her quaint, cottage-style house on Elm Street, but instead veered sharply towards an abandoned industrial complex on the dusty, forgotten outskirts of town, a hulking, dilapidated structure locals vaguely referred to as "The Old Mill." The sickly green glow, faint but unmistakable, pulsed rhythmically from within its decaying walls, a beacon of alien presence.

Hearts pulsating against their chest wall like trapped birds, they crept closer, hiding behind a collapsed concrete wall overgrown with tenacious weeds, the air thick with the smell of rust and damp concrete. Through a gaping, broken window, they saw it: a massive, perfectly symmetrical disc-shaped craft, its metallic surface shimmering with an unearthly luminescence, pulsating with the same eerie green light that had filled the assembly hall. And moving around it, in various stages of undress from their human facades, were their teachers. Their skin shimmered, their limbs elongated into grotesque, non-human proportions, their bodies shifting and reforming. Their eyes glowed brighter, more intensely than any human could sustain, alien fires within alien forms. Ms Davies, her face now a grotesque, insectoid parody of her human self, her delicate features stretched and distended, was overseeing a line of silent, transparent figures—the same kind Noah had seen in his fleeting glimpse of Jessica and Alex during the abduction, but these were older, more faded, their despair palpable, etched into their very transparent essence. They were being loaded onto the ship, shuffled forward like inert cargo, their forms almost merging with the green light.

The sheer, unfathomable alien horror of it seized them, freezing them in place. The adults they had known, the familiar faces they had trusted every day, were merely shells, meticulously crafted disguises for something ancient, terrifying, and profoundly malevolent. This wasn't just abduction; it was a horrifying, systematic harvesting of human essence, facilitated by entities that had infiltrated every aspect of their lives. The trust these teens had placed in their teachers, in the very institution of their school, in the adults who were supposed to protect them, shattered into a million icy fragments, leaving them adrift in a sea of pure terror. They felt utterly, terrifyingly alone.

A glint of light, reflecting off something metallic inside the mill, caught Liam's eye, drawing his attention to a new, more terrifying development. Principal Albright, her true form now fully revealed as a towering, multi-limbed insectoid creature, all sharp angles and chitinous plates, with multiple, faceted glowing eyes, was speaking to Mr Evans, who had transformed into a lean, scaly reptilian being, his tongue flicking out occasionally. "The resistance from the younger subjects is negligible," she hissed, her voice a series of chilling, complex clicking sounds that somehow translated into English directly into their minds, a telepathic invasion. "The programming holds. Soon, the new batch will be ready for the final transfer."

"New batch?" Chloe gasped, a raw, choked, terrified sound, her hand flying to her mouth to stifle any further noise.

It hit them with the force of a physical blow, a revelation that extinguished any remaining flicker of hope. They were the new batch. The abductions weren't finished; they were just beginning, accelerating. And they were next. Their time was running out, perhaps already gone. The school wasn't a place of learning; it was a farm, a breeding ground. And they, the students, were merely the crop, cultivated for some unspeakable purpose.

A stray pebble, dislodged by Noah's trembling foot, clattered loudly against the concrete floor, shattering the terrifying silence. The Principal's many, faceted eyes swivelled instantly, focusing with an unblinking, horrifying intensity on their hiding spot. A collective, unearthly growl, a sound that was both mechanical and organic, rose from the transformed teachers, a chorus of alien rage. There was no escape now, only the terrifying realisation that they were caught, completely surrounded by the monsters who had been their mentors, their guardians, their trusted adults, all along. The green light pulsed faster, intensified, and the deafening hum returned, promising not learning, not safety, but oblivion. The final bell, they knew, was about to ring, and this time, it wouldn't be for dismissal. It would be for forever… an unexplained abduction.

Chapter 29

The Echo Chamber of Lena's Mind

The world outside Lena's head was a blurry, distorted photograph, always just out of focus, always a step removed from reality. It wasn't a hallucination, not exactly. It was more like living behind a pane of warped glass, where every voice sounded a little off-key, every colour slightly muted, and every action she took felt as if someone else were pulling the strings. Her own thoughts echoed, twisted and amplified, inside a skull that felt less like a container and more like a vast, empty chamber. Trapped. The word vibrated in the hollow space behind her eyes, a constant buzzing static that filled her silent moments. She could see people, hear them, even reply, but the connection was tenuous, like a ghost reaching for a solid object.

This internal disconnect began subtly, a faint motion in the background of her consciousness. But as the school term wore on at Northwood college, a fortress of brick and blandness where uniformity was king, the sense intensified. It started with small, unsettling glitches around her. During Miss Kinder's perpetually cheerful assembly, the space around Lena's head would shudder violently whenever the principal's voice reached a certain grating pitch, plunging Lena's section of the hall into momentary shadow before snapping back to blinding brightness. No one else seemed to notice the targeted nature of the shudders In the chaotic bustle of the dinner hall, a stack of trays once tumbled, crashing loudly, right as a wave of frustration, thick and suffocating, washed over Lena. Her classmates blamed a clumsy year 7. Lena, however, felt a strange, cold vibration in her fingertips as they fell, a chilling echo of the impact.

Her internal trap wasn't just isolating; it was becoming a cage that rattled the world. The whispers in her mind, once indistinct, sharpened into a cacophony of urgent, conflicting voices. They weren't her own thoughts, not entirely. They were distorted echoes of conversations she'd barely registered, twisted into nonsensical commands, or sometimes, fragments of static that sounded like choked laughter. She'd find herself walking down a corridor, intending to go to her locker, only to realise her feet had led her to the library, her body acting without conscious direction. Her own voice, when she spoke, sometimes sounded like a stranger's, high-pitched and reedy, startling her as much as it did her friends. Chloe, her best friend, would often ask, "Lena, are you okay? You just zoned out." Lena would nod, feigning normalcy, but inside, she was screaming, unheard, against the walls of her mind.

The chaos escalated, becoming overt and undeniably strange. It wasn't just flickering lights and falling objects anymore. During a chemistry lesson, as Lena stared blankly at a complex equation, her frustration boiling into a silent, desperate roar within her skull, the Bunsen burner on her desk suddenly flared, the flame leaping impossibly high, singeing the ceiling tile above. Mr Harrison, usually stern, jumped back, his eyes wide with a mix of fear and suspicion as he looked at Lena. A few days later, during an important presentation in history class, Liam's carefully crafted digital display—a masterpiece of intricate animations—suddenly glitched. The screen filled with distorted static, then bizarre, pixelated symbols flickered across it, accompanied by a deafening screech from the speakers. Lena, seated in the front row, felt a surge of raw, unfocused power pass through her, a shudder that seemed to ripple from her core outward. Liam cursed, restarting his laptop, but the teachers' eyes, especially those of Principal Kinder, were now fixed on Lena with a new, unnerving intensity, a blend of concern and cold suspicion.

Students began to feel it too. Whispers followed Lena in the hallways, hushed theories about her "bad luck" or "creepy vibes." Small electronic devices—phones, calculators, even wristwatches—would sometimes spontaneously die or act erratically when she was near, as if her presence scrambled their circuits. The air around her sometimes felt inexplicably colder, raising goosebumps on nearby skin, a phantom chill in the otherwise warm school. Lena herself was terrified. She felt like a walking disaster, a magnet for mishap, but it wasn't her doing it. She was merely a passenger, a horrified observer trapped behind her eyes as her unseen tormentor caused havoc. The voices in her head grew louder, mocking her helplessness, sometimes even whispering commands she couldn't understand but somehow, horrifyingly, seemed to translate into real-world events.

The climax arrived during the annual school fair, a vibrant, chaotic explosion of student projects, games, and performances held in the packed main hall. Lena, volunteering at the "guess the number of jelly beans" booth, felt the pressure building. The noise, the crowds, the bright, dizzying lights—it was all too much for her already fractured perception. The internal static became a roaring tempest, the voices screaming, pulling, tearing at the edges of her sanity. She clutched her head, her eyes wide with a terror that had nothing to do with the outside world. Then, the world around her shattered.

A sudden, earth-shaking tremor ran through the entire building, not like an earthquake, but a sickening vibration that originated from the centre of the hall, from Lena herself. All at once, every overhead light exploded with a deafening pop, showering glass onto the terrified crowd. The sound system, blaring pop music moments before, twisted into a guttural, demonic roar, a distorted cacophony that ripped through the air. Project displays toppled, their wires sparking wildly. Booths crashed down, sending candy and prizes scattering. Panic erupted, a wave of screams and shoving bodies. Principal Kinder's voice, normally so calm, shrieked through the chaos, unrecognisable.

Lena was at the epicentre, her hands still pressed to her temples, her body convulsing, tears streaming down her face. She was screaming, but no sound escaped her lips; it was all trapped within that echo chamber. The air around her crackled with unseen energy, and fragments of the gym seemed to warp and shimmer, mirroring the distortions in her mind. Her eyes, wide and unfocused, seemed to look through the screaming faces, as if she was seeing something else entirely, something beyond the physical realm. The chaos was undeniable, inexplicable, and utterly terrifying.

Amidst the ensuing pandemonium—the wail of fire alarms, the shouts of teachers trying to restore order, the stampede of students—Lena simply vanished. One moment, she was there, a conduit of chaos, convulsing amidst the debris. The next, her space was empty, marked only by shattered glass and a lingering cold spot on the floor. No one saw her leave. No one saw her carried away. She simply wasn't there. Her jacket was found crumpled beneath a collapsed science project, her backpack still leaning against the jelly bean booth.

The official explanation was a "mass panic incident compounded by faulty wiring," a story the school administration clung to with desperate tenacity. The school fair was cancelled indefinitely. But the students and teachers who were there, who had seen Lena at the heart of the maelstrom, knew better. They spoke in hushed tones of the girl who had seemed to fall apart from the inside out, whose internal struggle had torn apart the very fabric of their mundane reality. Lena was never found. The mystery of her disappearance, and the source of the terrifying chaos that had preceded it, remained unsolved. Was she finally free from the prison of her own mind, or had the darkness within finally consumed her, pulling her into a psychotic abyss from which there was no return? Northwood school, once a place of predictable routines, now forever held the chilling memory of the day Lena's inner world exploded outward, leaving only emptiness in its wake.

Chapter 30

The Tide Pool Terrors

The salt spray hit Maya's face first, a cool, invigorating slap that chased away the last vestiges of geometry equations and the stuffy confines of Southreach College. Beside her, Liam wrestled a giant inflatable shark out of the boot of his beat-up sedan, his boisterous laugh echoing across the deserted stretch of sand, a joyful sound that instantly lifted her spirits.

Kelly was already spreading out their absurdly large, floral-patterned beach blanket, meticulously arranging an array of carefully packed snacks – artisanal crackers, organic fruit, and no fewer than three types of hummus. Meanwhile, Noah, always the first into the water, had practically vanished into the shimmering waves, a dark, rapidly diminishing speck against the glittering expanse of the ocean.

It was their annual "post-finals freedom" trip, a cherished ritual, this year to a supposedly secret beach known only through whispered rumours and a series of convoluted directions found on an obscure online forum. It was a perfect escape from the college and its endless, soul-numbing nature, a place where the world beyond them seemed to momentarily cease to exist. The sun beat down, a benevolent golden warmth, the gulls cried overhead in their timeless, mournful calls, and for a glorious few hours, nothing mattered but the rhythmic crashing surf and the sheer, intoxicating joy of being seventeen, untethered, and blissfully unaware of the horrors that lurked just beyond the horizon.

As twilight began to paint the sky in hues of fiery orange, soft rose, and deepening purple, streaking the southern horizon, a strange, profound silence fell over the beach. The familiar evening chirps of unseen insects, the distant croak of frogs, the gentle lapping of the tide – all were eerily absent, replaced by an unsettling stillness that pressed in on them.

A low, rhythmic chant, faint but distinctly audible, drifted on the breeze, seeming to come from the jagged, ancient cliffs that scarred the far end of the cove – a place they'd been vaguely warned away from by rusted, faded signs half-buried in the sand. "Did you guys hear that?" Kelly said, pulling her knees to her chest, her earlier meticulousness replaced by a visible tremor. Liam, usually quick with a joke or a sarcastic retort, just shrugged, a nervous tremor betraying his forced nonchalance. Tony, back from the water, his hair dripping, was suddenly rigid, his eyes fixed on a flicker of movement among the deepening shadows of the cliff face, his tanned skin now noticeably pale.

Then, the shadows moved. Not just shifted with the breeze or the fading light, but coalesced. Figures emerged from the gloom, distinct yet indistinct, cloaked in dark, heavy robes that seemed to absorb the very light, making them appear as holes in the twilight. Their faces, what little could be seen beneath deep, cavernous hoods, were blurred, indistinct, almost as if they were perpetually out of focus, or perhaps, not entirely human. But their movements were unnervingly synchronised, a silent, gliding advance that seemed to swallow the distance between them with impossible speed.

They carried no visible weapons, no glint of metal or sharp points, yet an aura of profound, ancient menace radiated from them, a chilling cold that seemed to seep into the very air. Panic, cold and sharp as a shard of ice, pierced through the teens' sun-drenched euphoria. "Run!" Liam finally managed to yell, his voice hoarse with terror, but it was already too late.

Before their feet could even scramble into motion, before their brains could fully process the impossible reality before them, the cloaked figures were upon them, silent as spectres, moving with prctcrnatural speed. There was a sudden, dizzying push, a chilling touch that felt less like hands and more like pure frostbite radiating into their skin, a sensation that stole their breath, and then the world went utterly, terrifyingly black.

They woke to a suffocating, absolute darkness, the air thick with the cloying smell of damp earth, stagnant water, and something acrid, like old blood mixed with ozone. Kelly was the first to whimper, a small, choked sound that echoed unnaturally in the confined space. They were in separate, cramped cells, each barely large enough to lie down in, made of rough, cold, unyielding stone that radiated a bone-deep chill. There were no visible bars, just heavy, impenetrable walls that seemed to press in on them, and a single, small, grated opening at the very top of each cell, high above their reach, offering no glimpse of the outside world.

The only light came from faint, greenish bioluminescent moss clinging to patches on the ceiling, casting eerie, shifting shadows that danced like tormented spirits on the stone. This wasn't a prison in any conventional sense; it felt like a tomb, an ancient, forgotten dungeon. Footsteps echoed in the unseen corridor outside, slow and deliberate, accompanied by murmurs in a language they didn't understand – a series of clicks and low tones that resonated with the stone.

A small, heavy hatch clanged open at the bottom

of Tony's cell, a harsh metallic scrape, and a shallow, stone bowl was shoved through. It contained a thick, grey gruel, completely odourless and utterly unappetising, its texture reminiscent of cold, wet ash. It was the same for all of them, delivered in the same dehumanising manner. They weren't being treated like prisoners to be interrogated or punished. They were being treated like specimens in a sterile, chilling laboratory. Like animals in cages.

The dehumanisation was relentless, a psychological assault as potent as any physical pain. Days blurred into a horrific, indistinguishable cycle, marked only by the arrival of the repulsive gruel. Food, always the same tasteless slop, was delivered with absolute silence, often shoved through the hatch with a rough, impersonal shove, as if they were indeed dogs in kennels, unworthy of even a glance.

There was no conversation from their captors, no eye contact, no acknowledgement of their screams or pleas, only the rhythmic thud of their heavy footsteps and the low chants that sometimes filled the air, reverberating through the solid stone.

They were forced to relieve themselves in a corner of their cells, the stench gradually adding to the oppressive, claustrophobic atmosphere, a constant reminder of their reduced state. The cult members, when they occasionally appeared during their "feeding" or what felt like "inspections," wore simple, unadorned robes, their faces always obscured by deep hoods, but their eyes, when caught in the dim light, were unnervingly bright, gleaming with an unnatural phosphorescence. They would simply stand there, observing, sometimes for minutes, sometimes for hours, their stillness absolute, taking notes on strange, opaque tablets that glowed with the same eerie green light as the moss.

They poked and prodded them with long, chillingly cold metal instruments, taking samples of blood, hair, skin, even saliva, always with the same detached, clinical precision, as if Maya, Liam, Kelly and Tony were merely biological units, data points in a horrifying equation, not terrified teenagers experiencing unimaginable trauma.

The silence, broken only by the incessant, unseen, incomprehensible machinery, was worse than any screams. It amplified every creak of the ancient stone, every drip of unseen water, every frantic beat of their own hearts, trapping them inside their own terror. They yearned for human contact, for a familiar voice, for anything that reminded them of who they were before this nightmare.

The cult was systematically stripping them of their humanity, reducing them to primal, instinct-driven beings, their identities slowly eroding under the constant pressure. Sometimes, a strange, sweet, cloying gas would filter into their cells through unseen vents, making them lightheaded, dizzy, and dulling their senses, leaving them lethargic and utterly compliant for hours, their minds hazy, their wills weakened.

One "day," indistinguishable from any other in the perpetual gloom, a different smell pervaded the air – metallic and sweet, like burnt sugar and fresh blood. It grew stronger, coating their tongues. The unseen machinery intensified, escalating from a low drone to a throbbing roar that vibrated through the very bedrock beneath them, making their teeth chatter. The cult members moved with a feverish, almost manic energy in the unseen corridors, their chants rising in pitch and urgency, a crescendo of sounds. This was it. The culmination. The experiment.

They were pulled from their cells, one by one, with a sudden, jarring roughness. Liam first, his desperate grunt echoing. Then Kelly, her muffled sob tearing at Maya's heart. Then Tony, his struggles quickly subdued. Maya was last, dragged roughly by two robed figures, their grip cold and firm, her bare feet scraping painfully against the cold, damp stone floor of the corridor.

They were brought into a vast, cavernous chamber, far larger than any school gym, its high ceiling lost in shadow. It was dimly lit, primarily by more of the pervasive green bioluminescent moss, but also by pulsing, alien machinery that ticked with a dangerous, unstable energy, throwing grotesque shadows across the rough-hewn walls. In the centre of this dreadful space stood a massive, circular platform, its surface smooth and dark, surrounded by intricate, glowing symbols etched into the floor, pulsing with the same unsettling green light. Liam, Kelly, and Tony were already there, strapped to individual restraints on the platform, their faces contorted in terror, their bodies twitching uncontrollably. Their skin seemed to shimmer faintly under the green light, and their eyes, Maya noticed with a gasp of horror that caught in her throat, held the same unsettling, internal luminescence that had radiated from their captors on the beach.

"The conduits are primed," a voice intoned, low and resonant, yet undeniably alien. It was unlike any human voice, a vibration more than a sound, yet perfectly comprehensible, a chilling telepathic intrusion. It seemed to come from a figure standing at the head of the platform, slightly taller and more imposing than the others, its hooded face tilted towards them, radiating cold authority. "The essence is ready for transfer. The transformation begins. The new vessels will be complete."

Suddenly, the air crackled with raw, uncontrolled energy, thick with ozone. The machinery shrieked, a sound of agony and raw power, an unbearable metallic scream. The green lights pulsed wildly, turning blinding, then dim, then blinding again, a strobe of pure, unfiltered terror. The cult members, who had been standing in precise, unmoving formations around the platform, their robes unruffled, began to convulse violently. Their heavy robes rippled, not from movement, but from grotesque, impossible distortions beneath. Flesh seemed to melt, bones to shift and crack with sickening, tearing sounds, audible even over the screeching machinery. High-pitched, inhuman shrieks, not of pain but of raw, primal, alien agony, erupted from them as their forms twisted into unimaginable, impossible shapes, limbs elongating, skin bubbling, eyes exploding into wider, multi-faceted glows that pulsed with chaotic light. The experiment wasn't working. It was going catastrophically, horrifically wrong, consuming its very orchestrators.

Liam screamed, an animalistic sound, as his restraints snapped with an audible crack, his body thrashing violently, no longer in control. Kelly's eyes rolled back in her head, and a thin, luminescent stream of green light pulsed from her mouth, her body spasming as if wracked by an invisible current. Tony began to convulse, tearing at the straps that held him, his movements jerking and unnatural, his limbs stretching and contracting with sickening elasticity. The air filled with the stench of ozone, scorched flesh, and something indescribably foul, a scent of corruption. The creatures that had been the cult members were no longer recognisable; they were dissolving into pools of shimmering, multi-coloured goo or exploding into bursts of green light and viscous, alien matter, their horrifying transformation consuming them entirely.

Maya, her own restraints suddenly loose, the unseen bonds shattered by the raw, unstable energy saturating the chamber, stared in abject horror. This wasn't just a physical experiment; it was something that altered the very essence of being, of consciousness, of life itself, and it had backfired spectacularly on its creators, becoming a self-destructive feedback loop. The platform beneath her vibrated violently, threatening to shake itself apart. She felt a strange tingling in her fingertips, a growing pressure behind her eyes, and then, a sudden, inexplicable surge of primal strength, a cold, surging power that hummed through her veins. The fear, the trauma, the sheer, unimaginable horror of witnessing her friends' grotesque transformation, fuelled a desperate, overwhelming will to survive.

She scrambled off the platform, her legs unsteady, navigating a nightmare landscape of melting bodies, convulsing machinery, and bursts of alien light. Liam, still thrashing, was slowly beginning to flatten, his form losing its three-dimensionality, becoming like a bizarre, writhing cardboard cutout. Kelly was a glowing, distorted silhouette, her form expanding and contracting, a terrifying, ephemeral lantern.

With a final, desperate surge of adrenaline, Maya crashed through a flimsy, half-rotted wooden door at the far end of the chamber, its ancient stone giving way like brittle paper under her unexpected, desperate strength. She ran, not knowing where she was going, fuelled by a raw, animalistic instinct to escape the dying screams of the cult and the horrifying, silent transformations of her friends. She didn't look back, even as the desperate, guttural cries faded behind her, replaced by the frantic thumping of her own heart and the strange, heightened whispers of her altered senses. She eventually found a narrow, winding tunnel that led upwards, its rough walls scraping against her. She emerged disoriented, stumbling onto the familiar, yet now utterly alien, moonlight of the beach. The air was clean, fresh with the scent of salt, but the stench of ozone, scorched flesh, and the lingering psychic echoes of the horror clung to her, an invisible shroud. She was free, but irrevocably changed, a sole survivor of an unspeakable terror, haunted by what she had seen and what she now felt bubbling within her.

The beach, once a haven of carefree joy, was now a place of silent dread, and the memory of her friends' final, horrific moments would haunt her forever. The cult was gone, consumed by their own twisted ambition, leaving only the chilling void of their disastrous experiment behind, and Maya, forever marked by its failure.

Acknowledgements

Cherry Sweet

Peter Darnes

Nick Ashton

Mielé & Koa

All Readers

Production Professionals

Development Support: Lucy Waite

All liaison's, friends and book supporters who helped in the
creation of this book and associated releases.

With Thanks

Discover more books, about the author - by web search.

LEON MITCHELL

Printed in Great Britain
by Amazon

12ba0406-5e1d-4b9a-8b7c-074a1b36e115R01